CALE

WALK OF SHAME #3

VICTORIA ASHLEY

CALE
Copyright © 2015 Victoria Ashley

Cover by: CT Cover Creations
Photographer: Simon Barnes
Model: Daniel Pollard
Edited by: Charisse Spiers
Formatting by: Perfectly Publishable

PROLOGUE
Cale

SIX YEARS AGO . . .

GRABBING RILEY BY THE WAIST I fall backward, pulling her into the freezing water with me. I feel her stiffen in my arms and squeal as the frigid water surrounds us, numbing our skin, as we slowly sink to the bottom with me still holding onto her. She's leaving for Mexico tomorrow and this might be our last moment together. The thought causes my chest to ache as I pull her even closer while we break through the water's surface, both of us fighting for air, and our bodies frozen.

She sucks in a deep breath before releasing it and screaming, "CALE!" Turning around in my arms, she presses her hands against my chest and shoves me, while trying to keep her teeth from chattering. "The water is free . . . eezing."

Her body is shaking violently from the cold, so I use this as an excuse to keep her warm. I've had feelings for Riley for as long as

I can remember, but timing has never seemed to be on our side. If I can't have her . . . then I'll wait. She means more to me than any woman ever could, and I have a plan to show her that—a promise that I made to myself. I just don't know how to tell her I want her without ruining our friendship, but I'll show her when the time is right.

Placing one arm behind her head, I pull her body against my chest and then wrap both of her legs around my waist as I back up against the wall of the pool to support her. "I've got you, Rile." I brush her wet, brown hair out of her face and smile as I reach out and touch her quivering bottom lip. I have to admit, she's so damn adorable while freezing her ass off. I should feel bad for torturing her, but I don't. Not really. I know she loves me teasing her. "If you don't stop shaking that lip . . . I'm going to bite it."

I see a hint of a smile, before she punches my chest and laughs. "You can be such a dick sometimes, Cale."

"I know," I admit. "That's why you love me so much, Riley Raines."

All laughter and playfulness seems to stop as our eyes meet. It looks as if she wants to say something, but stops right as her mouth opens to speak. Her face looks guilty and I hate it. I hate that look.

"What, Riley?" I pull her chin up as she looks away. "Say it," I whisper. "You know you can tell me anything."

She closes her eyes for a moment before shaking her head and biting her bottom lip. She looks hurt, but I have a feeling she won't give me the info I'm seeking. "It's nothing," she says softly. "It's just that . . . I'm going to miss you. That's all." She forces a smile and tugs on the ends of my hair playfully. "Don't look so sad, you big stud you. You'll do fine without me and forget about me in no time." She turns her head, hiding her eyes from my view.

"Not true. Don't *ever* say that." My heart is beating so damn hard against her chest that I'm surprised she hasn't asked me if I'm about to have some kind of freak attack. She's the only girl that makes my heart race like this and hearing those words out of her mouth causes it to ache like nothing else. How can she not realize how much I'm truly going to miss the shit out of her? "It's kind of hard not to be sad."

I make my best pouty face, trying to make her feel bad. This face always seems to work on her. "I have to wait for you to come home, all alone, so I can give you my virginity."

She looks stunned for a moment before she bursts out in laughter and squirms her way out of my arms. Her laugh is so damn beautiful. "You jerk. You almost made me feel bad for you for a minute . . . and we both know you're not a virgin. Stop kidding around." She attempts to pull herself out of the pool, but I grab her waist, stopping her.

"Where are you going?"

She looks down at me, water dripping down her beautiful curvy body. I want so much to just take her right here and give her all of me, but time is not on my side at the moment; it never seems to be when it comes to Riley. "It's getting late. I told my mom I'd be home early so I can finish packing."

"Stay," I whisper, pulling her back into the pool with me. My hands cup her face and I pull her so close that our lips are almost touching. "Don't leave me here."

"What?" She shakes her head and kisses me on the cheek, her lips lingering for a moment. "I can't. My grandma needs me. I have to go, Cale. I have no choice."

I watch as she gets out of the pool and grabs for my dry shirt, snuggling against it to keep warm, before pulling it over her head. I can't be sure, but it looks as if she sniffed it. I love that.

"I'm keeping this by the way." She smiles with a sad look in her eyes. "I'll be back. I promise. Time will fly by. Just watch." Her voice comes out sad and hesitant, because she and I both know that's not true. Time will definitely be a bitch while she's gone, and I'm sure it's going to feel like a lifetime without seeing her smile or hearing her beautiful laugh.

I nod my head and turn away from her as she starts walking away. I can't stand to watch her walk out of my life. It hurts more now that it's actually happening, especially knowing that there's nothing I can do to stop it, but . . . I need her to know one thing before she leaves. One thing that I hope will mean something to her in the future.

"I *am* still a virgin by the way," I say, wanting her to know I wasn't lying about that. I would never lie to Riley. I can't.

I hear her stop walking before I hear a small, but painful laugh. "Yeah, me too," she says. She whispers something afterwards but I miss it, too scared to look her way. I hear her footsteps in the grass as she starts walking again and it hurts so damn bad that I can't breathe.

By the time I get the courage to turn around she's gone . . . out of my life and soon she'll be out of Chicago. She's the one and only girl I have ever loved and I never even got the chance to tell her.

Life can be a bitch . . .

CHAPTER ONE

Cale

PRESENT DAY . . .

WALK OF SHAME IS FULL of people partying and getting wasted beyond sense, but really, I just can't seem to get my head into being here.

My mind has been on one thing and one thing only: Riley. Ever since Aspen blurted out that Riley would be home soon, my mind has been stuck on her. I've been replaying our last moment together, before she left, and it almost feels as if it were yesterday. The ache is still there, weighing on my chest.

We haven't spoken in over two years now, and even I know that I'm not over her. I'm not sure that I ever will be, and knowing that she's coming home reminds me of the promise I kept to myself six years ago, when I was still just a stupid teen.

We kept in contact for the first four years, talking on the phone at least once a week, late into the night, until she mentioned that she'd met someone that was interested in her. It hurt like hell, but knowing that she wouldn't be back home for a while I realized that I needed to let her live while she was there. There was no way I was going to hold her back by breaking down like a pussy and telling her how much I loved her. Asking her to wait for me as I have planned on waiting for her would be selfish.

Eventually, the calls slowed down until we were at the point that we barely talked but once every few months. Then . . . they ended all together. I think it was necessary in order for us both to go on with our lives, because every time we talked I could hear the ache and longing in her voice. I had to make it easier for *her* to live in hopes that it would make it easier for me.

Knowing that she'll be back any day now, possibly even now, has me unable to function properly.

I've been holding back from fucking other women, only giving them oral pleasure, because to me she's more important than just a meaningless lay. I thought that after we stopped calling each other every week that I would just forget about my promise to wait, but I never did. It's always been in the back of mind, fucking with me and making it impossible for me to take a woman to bed and give myself to her. I want her to find peace in knowing that when my cock enters her that she's the only woman I've been inside of and that I plan on pleasuring her over and over again until she can no longer handle me. I won't be able to stop and I sure as hell don't have any plans to.

Standing up straight, I run my hands through my hair while letting out a frustrated breath, bringing myself back to reality. I'm not much of a drinker, but right now . . . I feel like downing a fifth of whiskey.

Trying to get my head back into my performance, I twist both of my arms into the chain hanging above my head and thrust to the slow rhythm, while letting my unbuttoned jeans fall lower and lower with each movement. The screaming of the crowd causes me to put on a fake smirk and get into the moment as much as I will get, enough to at least finish my last performance of the night.

I'm close to the edge of the stage. Girls are reaching out to grope me as I give them a show. I can feel the sweat rolling down my body, dripping onto the marble stage at my feet as I continue pretending that I'm fucking every single girl in this room.

That's what they all want. That's *all* they ever want. These girls are here because they want to feel as if I want them, so . . . that's what I make them believe. As fucked up as it sounds, it sends them home happy. That's what matters here at *Walk Of Shame*.

"Right here! Cale!"

I open my eyes and bring them down to meet the brunette below me that is eagerly waving a wad of cash above her head. Releasing the chains, I walk to the edge of the stage, grab onto the back of her head, and grind my crotch into her face before thrusting repeatedly. In no time my jeans are on the floor and I'm standing in nothing but my white, very see through, boxer briefs.

I grind slow and hard, making her reach around and shove her cash into the back of my boxer briefs, just above my ass crack. I feel her hands exploring my ass, so I reach behind me and discretely pull them away before jumping off the stage.

The screaming of the women gets significantly louder as soon as my feet hit the main level. It's almost the end of my performance, and tonight I'm ending it with a little something special.

Making my way through the crowd I stop in front of the redhead that is hopefully going to help clear my head later. Straddling her lap, I sway my hips while running her hands up my bare chest, before pushing them down my body and stopping at the waist of my briefs.

I hear a little gasp escape her lips as I release her hands, letting her explore while I grind on her as if I were fucking her deep and hard; very deep and hard.

Smirking, I stand up from her chair before turning the other way and doing a quick handstand so that my cock is in her face. I begin to thrust my hips, swaying them around in a circle as the music speeds up, ending my performance.

All the women go wild as I grind my hips one more time and end it with a thrust to her face, before maneuvering my way back to my feet. Looking down at the ground, I focus on catching my breath, noticing all the cash surrounding me. Even with my head fucked up and lost somewhere else, my body still knows exactly what to do.

Walking away, I head over toward the back room to change, as Kash, the new kid, cleans up my stash of money. He showed up about a week ago asking for a job, so Lynx, the new owner, decided to make him our grunt for a few weeks first just to mess with him.

I'm standing here naked, just pulling a fresh pair of jeans on when I hear Kash step into the room and slap the pile of bills onto the table.

"Holy shit, bro." He slaps the money down a few more times and grins as I button my jeans and throw my white tee on. "Those girls are fucking insane. I've never seen such horny women in my life. This is a damn dream job. I swear my cock got grabbed at least five times just now."

Grabbing my tip money from Kash I grin and slap five twenties down into the palm of his hand. He hasn't seen shit yet. "Yeah, well you better be prepared to work that stage next week, rookie. You gotta learn to shake that cock of yours first. You've got some major shoes to fill."

He nods his head while stuffing the cash into his back pocket.

"I already know how to work it, bro. No worries."

"Alright, man." I slap his back. "I'm getting out of here. I'll see ya later."

"See ya," I hear him say right as I push my way back out into the crowd of women. It only takes me a few seconds to spot the sexy little redhead from earlier. She's watching me as if she's been waiting for me to come back out.

The cute little brunette that I was grinding on earlier is with her, sipping on her drink as they both eye fuck me all the way up to the bar.

Sara shakes her head and slides a draft beer across the bar top. "Damn Cale. I don't think I've ever seen you work it like that on the stage." She wipes her forehead off and waves her hand as if slinging sweat off of it. "So good tonight, baby."

I give her a half smile and reach for the frosty glass. "I have a lot on my mind tonight. I guess I was zoning out." I tip back the glass and let the refreshing liquid cool me off. I'm still sweaty from the show and all of my clothes are practically plastered to my wet body, irritating me.

"Yeah, well . . ." she tilts her head toward the right. "Those two girls definitely liked what you had going on tonight. It looks like they're about ready to rape you before you even get a chance to finish that beer off, babe." She rolls her eyes and dries off a glass. "Lucky dick. Those bitches are hot."

A few second later I feel a hand on each of my shoulders, before the brunette appears on my right and the redhead on my left. I don't even bother looking at them as I speak. "Ladies." I guzzle back my beer and toss down some cash for Sara. "Later, Sara."

Sara just waves me off as she gets called over by a small group of women. Shoving my wallet back into my jeans, I turn and walk through the crowded bar, not surprised to hear the sound of heels clicking against the floor behind me.

Yes, I could definitely use a very long blowjob right now, but to be honest, I could also do without. These two women, even combined, could never measure up to the woman that I have waited six long years for. I'm not saying that I'd turn them down, just saying that maybe I won't be seeking out tonight.

As soon as I step outside and head for my truck, I hear one of the girls call my name, stopping me. Leaning against my truck, I exhale and look up, while dangling my keys around my finger.

The redhead pushes her hand against my chest as the brunette leans in and whispers in my ear, "Let us take care of you, Cale." She runs the tip of her tongue over my earlobe before speaking again. "Just relax and enjoy."

Leaning my head back, I close my eyes and take in a small breath as my jeans get pulled to my knees, and then I feel two small hands grip around my ready cock.

A pair of soft lips wrap around my head as a hand runs up and down my shaft, and I know right away that both women are sharing right now. I'm not selfish. It's big enough for the both of them and maybe right now . . . this distraction . . . is what I need, so I let them both take turns sucking me off right here in the parking lot until I blow my load all over both of their mouths.

Licking the remainder of cum off my dick, the redhead stands up and places her arms around my neck. "Let us take you home where we can show you a *real* good time. I promise you that it will be worth it."

"More than worth it," the brunette chimes in.

That offer would usually have any man falling to his knees and drooling, but not me. I've gone twenty-four years without it and I'm pretty damn sure I can go another few weeks.

Trying my best not to be an ass, I take turns pressing my lips to both of their temples, before saying goodnight and hopping in my truck.

CALE

Once I pull up at the house, I realize that having my dick sucked hasn't done shit to clear my head. Riley Raines is coming home and I know without a single doubt that she's going to ruin me.

CHAPTER TWO

Riley

I'M SO NERVOUS RIGHT NOW. I've only been back in Chicago for two days and in about two seconds I'm starting my new job here at *Sensual Touches*, the massage parlor that I applied for online a few weeks ago.

No one knows that I'm back yet. I made sure to tell Aspen not to tell anyone until I'm ready. The only people that know are my family, and I plan on keeping it that way for a couple of weeks until things settle down and I can relax a bit. My heart is still hurting and my head is spinning out of control at the fact that Tyler and I are no longer a couple and that I have to get familiar with my surroundings again. When I made plans to move back home Tyler decided at the last minute that he didn't think he'd be up for the move . . . so he stayed behind.

I care about Tyler, but Chicago is where my heart is. Not to mention . . . it's where *he* is: Cale Kinley. As much as I've tried to convince myself seeing him again won't stir some crazy emotions inside of me, I know with everything in me that's not true. I'm not sure that I can handle seeing him while in this emotional state.

Shaking my head, I run my hands down my black, skinny jeans, wiping the sweat from my palms as I approach the door to the massage parlor. "It's no big deal, Riley. You've done this a million times before . . . just not here. You have magic fucking hands." I convince myself before stepping inside.

As soon as I enter the building I'm greeted by a woman that looks to be in her early twenties, with long, purple hair. She plasters on a smile and stands up from her chair, looking impatient. "Please tell me you're Riley Raines. Hailey hasn't shown up yet and we have two clients waiting. I need to get these two satisfied and hitting the road."

I nod my head as the nerves flow through me, causing butterflies to fill my stomach. "That's me," I say with a fake confidence that I definitely don't feel at the moment. "Is there anything you need from me before I start?" I open my purse and start digging for my ID and paperwork. "Here's my–."

"No time for that, sweetness. Myles will deal with that when he gets in later. I don't get paid enough for that." She gives me an impatient look and starts shoving me down the hall. "I need you in room three. That's your room." She takes a deep breath and bites her bottom lip. "You're going to enjoy this one. *Please* put your hands all over him since I can't. Hailey is going to be one pissed off bitch, but this will teach her a lesson for showing up late." She lets out a satisfied laugh while spinning on her heels. "Hurry. I can smell the skank coming now."

Lifting my eyebrows, I smile small and push open the door to room three, almost unable to breathe from the nerves. Without paying any attention to the waiting client, I quickly observe the room to find a chart hanging next to the door. I grab it quickly to prepare for his needs.

While searching for my supplies, I introduce myself, trying not to draw attention that I have no clue where anything is. "Sorry for the wait. My name is Riley and I'll be taking care of you today. Hailey is running a little behind and this is my first day here, so please be a little patient while I get everything ready."

Looking around the dimly lit room, I find the stereo and turn it on, letting the relaxing sounds fill the space to hide my erratic breathing as I try to stay calm. I've been at the same place for three years, and being somewhere new, with new clients, is a bit nerve-wracking; especially when you're getting rushed around by some chick with purple hair and tattoos that looks as if she wants to choke someone today.

After securing my apron filled with my lotions and oils, I turn to the table and my heart starts pounding like crazy in my chest as I see a body, barely covered by a small towel, just waiting to be touched by me. I swallow hard while letting my eyes roam over the stiff muscles of the tanned back on display. The top of the client's ass peeks out of the towel, displaying the roundest, firmest ass I have ever seen before . . . and the dimples in his back are making it hard for me to gain some much-needed confidence.

Doing a silly little shake in an attempt to shake my nerves off, I squirt some oil in my hands and slowly run my hands up the bottom of his back, being sure to make it feel as insanely good as I possibly can.

The feel of his muscled back beneath my fingers and the deep, undeniably sexy moan that escapes his throat almost has me turned on as I start to go lower, until I'm right above his ass.

"Go lower," the deep voice whispers. "Take the towel off."

I almost deny his request, when I remember that *Sensual*

Touches is clothing optional. That's the *one* thing that almost kept me from applying, but comparing the pay that you get here versus the other options, I knew what my choice had to be.

"This is new to me," I whisper, before speaking up. "Let me know if you get uncomfortable and I'll replace it before you flip over on your back."

"That won't be an issue," he says huskily.

Keeping my moan to myself, I lower my hands down to his ass, removing the towel little by little as I continue to get lower. As soon as my hands reach the bottom of his ass, I remove the towel completely and hold back the gasp that fights to escape me.

Holy hotness . . .

Remembering that this was per his request, and that it's fully professional to be doing this here at *Sensual Touches,* I grip the back of his upper thighs and massage it while rubbing my thumbs over the bottom of his tight ass, enjoying every single moment of it.

In fact, I'm enjoying it so much that I almost feel guilty. Tyler and I have been broken up for less than a week, and here I am enjoying myself as I rub on another man's ass, listening closely for each moan that he will grace my ears with.

After spending a good, long, fifteen minutes on his ass itself, I focus my attention on the rest of his muscular body, mentally preparing myself for the rest of his gloriousness that I'll be seeing in the *flesh* as soon as I finish up on his backside.

Now I understand why that Hailey chick is going to be pissed off. Massaging this stud has to be the best part of her job here. How can you *not* enjoy this?

Pulling my hands away, I turn away to give him some privacy. "I'm ready for you to flip over, sir. Please let me know when you're ready."

"I'm always ready for you, Rile."

Fighting to catch my breath, I place my hand to my heart and slowly turn around to see that the naked stud whose ass I have been ogling over this whole time is Cale. Cale Kinley. My Cale Kinley, the one person that I've been so worried about seeing again and now here he is, naked and in front of me.

"Cale," I whisper. "Holy shit. I don't . . . I don't know what to say. Wow. It's you. I . . ."

Sitting up, he smiles and grabs my hand, pulling me closer to him as if it were old times again. "Get the hell over here, woman." Pulling me into his arms, he hugs me tightly against him, while running his nose up the side of my neck. "I've missed you so fucking bad, girl."

Feeling overwhelmed, my eyes water a little bit as I hold him as tightly as I can. A smile spreads across my face as we pull apart and check each other out. Luckily, he didn't ruin me completely and decided to cover his junk up. "You look just like you did the last time I saw you, except a hell of a lot stronger and even hotter. Holy hell, you have grown up, Cale. I didn't even recognize your voice. My Cale is a man now."

He grabs me by the hip and squeezes. "Yeah . . . I guess you can say I've grown quite a bit." He flexes his jaw as he checks me out, completely taking me all in. His striking green eyes almost melt me on the spot as I watch them. "All of me."

I find myself swallowing hard and slightly sweating as I try to figure out what exactly he could mean by *all of him*. I think I know the answer to that and I have to admit that it has me turned on completely.

"You look fucking beautiful, Riley." He bites his bottom lip and releases his grip on my hip, letting his hands brush over my ass, before he grips my upper thighs. "So damn beautiful."

Without even thinking, I reach out and grip the blonde hair at the back of his neck. He wears it slightly shorter than he did six years ago, but still sexy as can be.

"I see you're still the same smooth talker," I say with laughter. "Good to know."

He grips my thighs tighter, pulling me closer to him. "And you're still the most beautiful woman I've ever laid eyes on."

Feeling myself come undone under his intense stare, I release his hair and reach for his hands, pulling them away from my thighs. "I've missed you, Cale." I watch him with a smile as his eyes follow my movements to my hands. I squirt a handful of oil into my palm.

His eyes take on a darkened look and he grabs my hands, placing them to his chest, and holding them there. "Why didn't you tell me you were back already?" He rubs his thumbs over my wrists, looking me dead in the eyes. "When did you get home?"

Letting out a small breath, I shake my head and begin rubbing my hands over his body while pushing him backward until he's lying flat on his back. "Only two days, Cale." I suck in a breath and try to hide the small moan as my hands explore every hard ridge of his chest and abs, attempting to continue his massage. God, this is torture right now. This is the kind of body that you only see in the damn movies. "I just wanted a week or so to get settled in first. No one knows that I'm back except for my family. You were going to be the next to know. I promise."

He smiles up at me and I can't help but to notice the way my heart skips a beat. That smile—seeing it right now is a painful reminder of what I've been missing for the past six years. The ache in my chest almost causes me to lose my composure, wondering what all I've missed while being away.

The only thing I've heard over the years is that he works at a bar. I don't even know if he has a girlfriend. For some reason, I just couldn't allow myself to know that bit of information, so I made Aspen promise to never tell me. Well . . . more like I threatened to choke the life out of her through the phone.

Now standing here, touching him and seeing his beautiful

smile, I can't help but want to know. Is he going home tonight to make love to some woman while she gets to put her hands on the places that I'm touching now? I don't want to know!

"Have dinner with me tonight."

A smile spreads over my face, unexpectedly from his request. It's so big that my face hurts, but I try my best to hide it so I don't look like a desperate loser. "Are you cooking me dinner, Chef Cale? If so, then I hope it's better than what I tasted the last time you attempted to cook for us," I tease, even though I'd eat dirt if it made him happy.

"Of course," he says confidently. "And it will definitely taste damn good. I promise you that the only things I'll put in your mouth are the things that I know will satisfy you completely and ruin you for anything else."

I swallow hard and try not to take that comment sexually, even though my body is definitely taking it *that* way. "Alright." I agree. "I'm trusting you with my mouth, so you better not disappoint."

He lifts his eyebrows and I can't help but to notice him harden beneath the towel, but I play it off as if I hadn't noticed. "You have no idea, Riley. You should be careful what you trust me with." Sitting up, he leans in and kisses me on the side of the mouth, his lips lingering for a few seconds too long. "I have an early shift at the bar today, but I'll get your number and address from Aspen."

"Alright." I smile. "I'll be here until six, but I'm free after that."

Nodding his head, Cale jumps up from the table, allowing his towel to drop as he reaches for his clothes to get dressed. I somehow manage to turn away before I get to see what I've been longing to see since we were in high school. Damn, I really hate myself right now.

I hear a small chuckle from Cale before I feel his hands wrap around my waist and his lips press against my neck from behind. "Gotta go, baby. Be ready for me tonight."

Next thing I know, Cale is out the door, and I'm standing here fighting to catch my breath. "Baby . . ." I say softly. I have to admit I like being called that by Cale. That's definitely new.

Being back is going to be a bigger challenge than I thought . . .

CHAPTER THREE
Cale

THERE'S ONE MORE HOUR BEFORE my shift ends and I'm feeling so restless that I can barely pay attention to the drinks being ordered. Hemy and I are working the bar while Stone is busy with the girls on the floor. I have to admit that the dude has skills.

I wasn't sure if he'd be able to fill Slade's shoes, but I'm pretty damn impressed at how crazy and out there he is with his abilities.

I look away from the crowd of crazy women, when I'm caught off guard with an elbow as it jabs me in the ribs. "What the shit?"

Turning beside me, I look up to see Hemy glaring at me. "What the fuck are you doing, staring off and shit? I'm working my dick off over here."

Ignoring his ass, I quickly snap out of it and focus on the steady flow of drinks that keep getting requested, trying my hardest to not think about Riley and how fucking fantastic it felt having her hands on my body. Truthfully, I wanted them *all* over, but I don't think she's ready for that quite yet, so I'm doing my best to respect her and take things slow. Well, as slowly as I can.

As soon as I get a free moment, I pull my phone out and send Slade a quick text, asking him to get Riley's number from Aspen. At first Slade texts back with a big FUCK YOU, before he sends another message about five minutes later, telling me he had to wrestle with Aspen to get her phone and that I owe his ass.

He's just lucky that he's my guy and that I know how much of an ass he is and still tolerate him. I have to admit that he's gotten about eighty percent better since meeting Aspen, so really, I owe *her*.

Leaning against the register, I send Riley a text, ignoring the screaming crowd for a moment. There's no way she's getting out of spending the night with me. I don't care if I have to throw her over my shoulder and handcuff her to me for the night. I've missed the shit out of her and tonight . . . she's mine.

> Me: Hey, baby. Where am I picking you up tonight? I hope you save room for dinner and dessert, because I'm ready to work magic with my hands . . .

My phone vibrates a few minutes later, causing me to turn away from the girl chatting my ear off at the bar. She's still talking as I read Riley's message.

> Riley: Magic, huh? So you're that good? ;) Don't even answer that. I'll be the judge of that later. Pick me up at my mom's around seven. I'll be ready and waiting . . .

Damn girl . . . She has no idea what she's just started.

I adjust my cock and hope my boner will quickly go down. The last thing I need is something to set these women off. I barely make it through a shift as it is without getting attacked with a set of tits in my face. I don't need anything slowing me down tonight.

"Are you free tonight?" Biting my bottom lip, I shove my phone in my pocket and shake my head at the girl in front of me, before letting her down as easily as I can.

"Sorry, beautiful, but I'm taken for the night." I slide a free drink across the bar as a look of disappointment takes over her face. "The drink is on me."

She smiles small and reaches for the drink, not doing much to hide her sour face. "Just let me know when you're free." With that, she turns and walks away, swaying her hips in the process. I know without a doubt that she's trying to lure me in, but that shit isn't working on me, especially when the woman that I've waited six years for is within my reach.

She's about to finally see how much I truly want her . . .

CALE WILL BE OUTSIDE ANY minute, and for some reason that thought has me extremely nervous and sweaty. Why am I so nervous when this is the guy that I spent most of my teen years with? He's still the same guy, except . . . he's drop dead gorgeous and every inch of his body is covered in hard muscle that I want nothing more than to explore with my tongue.

This new desire stirs me up, making it hard for me to act normal and pretend that I don't crave to be with him. It seemed a lot easier six years ago when I saw him almost every day, but after being away from him for so long, seeing him just brings back all of my old feelings on top of the ache that I felt when I could no longer spend my days with him.

I shake my head. "Doesn't matter, Riley," I whisper. "Just act normal." I rub my sweaty palms down the side of my black dress and take in a deep, calming breath. "He's still the same sweet Cale that wants nothing more than to be friends. Just friends . . ."

I hear a noise in the hallway that causes me to look up and walk toward my bedroom door. My parents went out to dinner after I told them that I had plans, so I've been here alone for the last thirty minutes.

"Aspen," I call out. "Is that you? I'm in my old bedroom."

I hurry into the hallway and slam into a hard body, almost causing me to stumble backward, but Cale catches me with a grin. His arm tightens around my waist as his smile broadens. "You look hot, Rile." He leans in and kisses me on the forehead, before pulling me straight up and back on my feet. "You ready to go?"

I tug on the end of my skirt, pulling it down, and then smile, as Cale looks me over with wide eyes, whistling softly. "I've missed you, Cale. You seriously have no idea." I laugh as he grabs my arm and spins me around as if checking me out. It's something he used to do to me when he would first see me for the day. I know he's doing it now to make me feel comfortable and I love him for it. It reminds me of how strong our friendship was and why I adored him so much.

"Let's go." He nods his head and places his hand on the small of my back, guiding me through the house. "I have dinner in the oven."

I step outside and watch him as he locks the door and closes it behind him. "Oh really?" I smile big at the thought of Cale cooking. I thought he was only kidding. "You're really cooking us dinner?"

He wraps his arm around my waist and pulls me against him as we walk to his truck. "Hell yes I am. I owe you after all those times you cooked for me while we were hanging out at your house. At my house, I will always cook you dinner, especially if it keeps you coming back for more." He winks and helps me into his truck.

He refuses to tell me what's for dinner on the way over to his house, even though I made it a point to ask him every few minutes, just to see if he'd cave. I almost forgot just how strong Cale's willpower is. He's pretty set once he makes his mind up. He's always been the strongest person that I know and I admire him for that, even though it sometimes has the power to annoy the shit out of me.

He jogs over and helps me out of his truck once we pull up to his house. "You'll be spending a lot of time here, Rile, so I hope you like it just as much as I do." I laugh and he raises a brow in question. "What? You don't believe me?"

"What makes you think that I'll like you as much as I used to?"

He pushes the door open and pushes up behind me, guiding my body with his into the house. His lips brush my ear. "I have a pretty good feeling," he whispers. "You'll like me even more . . ."

Walking around me, he throws his keys onto the kitchen island and walks over to the oven with a confidence that makes me melt. "Make yourself at home, because you're spending the night. We're having a movie night and I'll take you home before eight in the morning to change for work."

This time, I'm the one lifting my brows. "How do you know what time I work tomorrow, *Cale*?"

He opens the oven and pulls a pan out, setting it on the stove. "Because I asked on my way out. You didn't think that I would be making all my future appointments without booking with you, did you? You're the only woman that I'll be getting a massage by from now on. I promise that."

I swallow hard and try to keep my nerves from jumping all over the place. He has no idea what his words are doing to me. He may not be trying, but they're definitely making me extremely *hot*.

I take a seat at the table when Cale refuses to let me help with anything, and within ten minutes the table is covered with food: baked chicken alfredo, breadsticks, salad, wine for myself, and beer for Cale.

Looking at all of the food makes my mouth water in anticipation. Cale cooked all of this knowing damn well that it's my favorite meal. I'll definitely owe him for this later and I'm positive he won't forget to collect. It's a good thing that I know practically all of his likes and dislikes. At least . . . I used to.

We don't talk much until we've both eaten a good amount and we're both on the verge of being stuffed. Cale must notice me slowing down, so he leans back in his chair and smiles up at me.

"So talk to me, Rile." He takes a swig of his beer and looks at me, ready to listen.

I take another huge bite of noodles, before licking my lips and smiling up at him. "About what?" I breathe out, feeling like I'm about to pop from overeating. "About how damn delicious this food is? Holy crap, Cale. This is so good. I'm very impressed."

He bites his bottom lip and leans in closer to me. "Told you I'd only put tasty things in your mouth." He shakes his head with a slight smile as my face undoubtedly turns beet red. "But I want to know about you. What's been going on? Where's the boyfriend? Why are you at your parents' house? That kind of stuff."

I take a huge drink of my wine and reach for the bottle to refill it. "We broke up before I left. It's a long story that I don't feel like talking about right now. I'm only staying with my parents until I can find my own place. Aspen offered to let me stay there, but I don't want to intrude on her and Slade." I take another drink and pretend to be unaffected. "I'm sure that I'll find a place soon and being back in Chicago will feel like home again. It will just take some time."

He looks me in the eyes for what feels like an eternity before he speaks. "Come stay with me."

I smile at his offer. "Thanks, but I don't know about that, Cale. My parents don't mind me staying there for a while. We haven't seen each other in six years and I don't want things to be awkward."

I stand up and get ready to clean up my mess, but Cale stops me and tells me to leave it on the table. "I'm not worried about that mess right now. What I'm worried about is spending time with you and there's no way in hell that things could *ever* be awkward between us. I don't care if it's been twenty years, we're still Rile and Cale and I always have the time and room for that in my life." He pulls me up from my chair and grabs my glass of wine. "Pick out a movie and I'll be there in a few minutes."

"Are you sure you don't—."

"Hell no, Rile. I invited you here for dinner. There's no way I'm allowing you to clean up." He pulls me by the back of the neck, until our faces are almost touching. "Now go to my room and find a pair of my boxer briefs and a shirt. I'll meet you on the couch."

I close my eyes and nod as his smell surrounds me. He smells so damn good that I just want to snuggle into him and run my nose all along his chest and neck. "Okay," I say softly.

Without warning, he releases my neck and walks over to the table to start cleaning up. I watch him for a second to try and imagine what it would be like living here with Cale. Seeing him every morning when I wake up and every night before bed. I have a feeling there's no way I could handle that without wanting more. Plus, it would kill me to see him bring other girls home. Cale truly has no idea how much I care about him and I'm hoping to keep it that way.

After slipping into some of Cale's clothes, I take a seat on the floor and search through his DVDs. I instantly spot a new comedy that I've been wanting to see, so I pop it into the PS4 and curl up on the corner of 'the couch to wait for Cale.

A few minutes later I hear Cale approaching, so I look up. Without a care in the world he yanks his shirt over his head before stepping out of his jeans, making my heart race with every movement that he makes.

He smiles at me when he notices me watching him. "I've been waiting to get out of these clothes all fucking day." With his abs flexing, he walks toward the couch and takes a seat, practically pulling me into his lap. He reaches for the blanket on the back of the couch and drapes it over us before pressing play with the controller. "You comfortable," he questions.

Yes . . . and no.

He isn't hard, but feeling his dick pressed against my ass definitely steals my breath for a brief second. There were so many times in the past that I wanted to feel him against me, but was too afraid to get close to him, so I always found ways to avoid contact with his junk. There's no way I would have been able to withstand begging him to take me, and right now . . . I'm fighting that urge.

"I'm fine." I lie. "Just let me know if you want me to move and I will."

He pulls me tighter against him and smiles into my neck. "I haven't seen you in six years. There's no way in hell that I'm letting you move away from me."

My heart beats faster from his words and I have to admit to myself that those are the exact words I wanted to hear. Being with him feels like old times and I'm happy to see that Cale wants me around just as much as in the past. I was scared things would be different . . .

I just hope that I can keep my feelings under control before I mess up everything we've had over the last ten years.

CHAPTER FOUR

Cale

RILEY FELL ASLEEP IN MY arms over two hours ago, but I haven't had the heart to move her so that I can get comfortable. She's sleeping like a damn baby, as if she's completely exhausted and hasn't slept in days. I can't even imagine how much of an effect this huge change must me taking on her both physically and emotionally.

Everything has changed dramatically for her in the last week. Her grandmother has gone off to a nursing home, she's packed up all of her things to move from the home she has known for the last six years, and on top of that has just gotten out of a relationship that I'm guessing was not by *her* choice.

I'll sit here all night if she's content and at home for the first time since she's left Mexico. She loves her parents, but there's no way she will be able to be herself there without having them on her ass constantly, making her feel as if she's a kid again; not to mention that she has to feel lonely there without someone she's close to. That's why my offer for her to stay here will always stand.

I feel her stir in my arms before she looks up at me with tired eyes and attempts to sit up. I pull her back into me and smile down at her as she begins to speak. "How long have I been sleeping?" She asks tiredly. "Sorry if I drooled on you."

I give her a small smile as she wipes her mouth. There's a wet circle of drool on my chest, but I could care less. "You're all good, Rile. Nothing that I haven't dealt with before from you." I help her stand up before I get to my own feet. "You dozed off a couple hours ago. I figured you needed the rest so I didn't want to wake you."

"Cale." She smiles at me gratefully and pulls me in for a tight hug. "You've always been so selfless when it comes to our friendship. I think I've missed that the most about you."

I smile against her neck. "Now why don't you go crawl into my bed and fall back to sleep. I'll take the couch for the night."

She pulls away from me and looks as if she wants to say something, but doesn't. She just turns away and starts heading for my bedroom, before stopping at the door and turning back around. "Night, Cale."

I turn off the lamp and strip out of my boxers, while holding the blanket against me. "Goodnight, Rile. I'll wake you up in the morning."

Her eyes linger down to my hand that is holding the blanket, before she nervously turns away and disappears into my bedroom.

I might have forgotten to mention the little fact that I *always* sleep naked. It was a struggle for me when Aspen and Slade were staying here, but as soon as they left I went back to my nudist ways.

If Riley agrees to stay here, then she's going to see me naked whether it's me running around the house or me on top of her, burying myself between those thighs of hers. I just hope that she's ready for me.

I've been more than ready for her . . .

THE ALARM ON MY PHONE woke me up at seven, not that I really slept much anyways. Having Riley sleeping in my bed kind of prevented that. I kept thinking about crawling into bed with her, but decided that it's probably too soon. There's no way I would've been able to lie next to her without wanting to pleasure her and make her scream until she fell asleep in my arms from exhaustion, so I spent most of the night fighting with my damn dick.

I quietly slip into my boxers and prepare a quick breakfast before waking Riley up. There's no way I'm sending her to work on an empty stomach.

I walk into my room to see Riley curled up in my bed, holding my spare pillow against her body for comfort. Every part of my body aches to be that comfort. It's probably been a while since she's slept alone, and seeing her having to use a pillow makes me want to show her what my body could do for her.

She looks so damn beautiful and peaceful, lying there in my clothes and bed, that I feel bad for having to wake her so early. A part of me just wants to crawl into my bed with her and say fuck everything else. Fuck *Sensual Touches* and fuck *Walk Of Shame*. I want Cale and Riley time and you better believe that I will be getting it as soon as I get off work tonight.

Just as I'm about to lean in and brush her beautiful, brown hair out of her face, she opens her eyes as if she can sense I'm next to her.

She stretches and smiles up at me, looking sweet and innocent. It makes me wonder just how innocent her sexy little body really is; although, I have a feeling that it hasn't been as innocent over the last six years as I'd hoped. "Morning." Sitting up, she looks around as if trying to figure out what time it is. "Did I over sleep? Shit!" She changes position in a panic, tossing the pillow aside.

"Hell no, Rile. I wouldn't let that happen. I got you." I reach for her hand and help her up to her feet. "Come eat so that I can take you home to shower and get ready for work."

She stops walking and gives me a funny look. "You cooked us breakfast?"

I give her a light slap on the ass to get her moving again. "No." I laugh as her eyes light up at the food on the kitchen island. "I made *you* breakfast. I hardly eat in the morning. Plus, it's early as hell, Rile. I'm never up this early." I lean against the fridge and cross my arms as she pulls out a stool and takes a seat. "I'm going back to sleep as soon as I drop you off. I have to work later tonight."

She holds up a pancake, before slapping it down onto her plate. "Thank you. You really didn't have to do all of this. I could have stopped for a quick sandwich on the way to work. That's what I usually do."

I shake my head. "You're in my house; therefore, I feed you. Now eat up."

It's silent for a few minutes while she eats, before she finally speaks up, breaking the comfortable silence. I bring a glass of orange juice to my lips. "You work at the bar tonight? Bartending, right?"

I choke a little on my orange juice, realizing that I haven't mentioned the small fact that I'm a fucking male stripper. The last time we had talked I was mostly bartending. I didn't think the stripping part was going to last.

I set my orange juice down and walk over to grab her empty plate, bringing it to the sink. "Why don't you go and change real fast and we'll talk on the way to your parents'."

She nods her head and sets her empty glass into the sink. "Good idea. I'm running out of time and I can't afford to lose this job if I want to find my own place soon."

I quickly dress and we both end up meeting by the front door in less than five minutes. Opening it for her, I lock the door before closing it behind us.

It feels so strange being outside at this time in the morning. It's so quiet and peaceful. I have to admit, I sort of like being up right now, and having Riley by my side makes it that much more enjoyable.

After helping her into my truck, I jog over to the driver side, mentally preparing myself for the bomb drop. I just hope that she can handle it without thinking any less of me. I never really cared what anybody thought about it until . . . *now*. She's always known me as the *sweet* Cale. I'm definitely far from her sweet Cale today, especially with my body.

She smiles and faces me as I pull out of the driveway and onto the road. "So . . . tell me about your job, Cale. I want to know what you've been up to. I want all the details."

I grip the steering wheel and grind my jaw, preparing for her reaction. There's really no way of sugarcoating this. I just have to come out and say it and hope that she accepts it. "I'm stripping tonight."

She lets out a small laugh as if she thinks I'm joking. "Stop playing around, Cale." She grabs my knee and squeezes it. "Really, tell me."

I stop at a red light and look over at her. I give her a serious look to show her that I'm not joking. "I've been stripping at *Walk Of Shame* for a while now. I only bartend a couple of nights a week now."

"Green light," she says quickly.

I turn away from her to pay attention to the road, just waiting for her to say something else. I want to know what she truly thinks about me now. I always want nothing but the truth from her and I always know that she'll give it to me straight.

"That's actually pretty cool. I bet you make a lot of money," she says, as if it's no big deal. "If you have the body, then hey . . . show it off. I can't imagine anyone complaining." She smiles at me and I feel a flood of relief wash through me.

"I haven't had any complaints yet."

She laughs. "Well obviously, Cale. You have the body of a God." She gives me a look that makes me want to rip her clothes off and fuck her right here. "I've always wanted to go and see male strippers. I've just never had the opportunity."

I lift an eyebrow. "You going to come and watch me one night then?"

She gently bites her bottom lip. "We'll see."

I pull into her parents' driveway and lean in to give her a kiss on the cheek. "I'll come pick you up when I get off work tonight. We still have *a lot* of time to make up for, and until then you're mine."

She huffs and glances at the house, looking as if she already wants to run away. "I'll be here, waiting. I'm off by four and I've been thinking about swinging by to see Aspen for a bit."

"Sounds good, Rile. Tell Aspen that she needs to come and see me soon. It's been too long."

"Will do." She smiles one more time before hopping out of the truck and walking away, stopping to smile back at me, before disappearing into the house.

Damn, this is going to be a long day.

CHAPTER FIVE

Riley

I'M JUST GATHERING UP MY things to leave work for the day when Hailey stops me by poking her head out of her door.

"Hey. Are you leaving?"

I nod my head and look down at the keys in my hand. "Yeah, I'm heading out right now. What's up?"

She gives me a sweet smile, obviously trying to butter me up for something. "I'm running a little behind and I have a client that's been waiting for like twenty minutes. Kylie has been on my ass and I can't handle her shit right now. Can you please take care of them so I can finish up?" She nods her head toward her door and whispers, "This suit pays a lot of money and he's not ready to leave yet. So?"

I look down at my phone in my hand to see that Aspen has

finally responded to my message. Holding up my finger to Hailey, I quickly check the message to see that Aspen won't be home until at least five thirty. I really have nothing better to do anyways.

"Yeah, I can do it. I'll tell Kylie to send them to my room."

Hailey flashes me a half smile, before disappearing back into her room.

"Yeah, you're welcome," I mutter to myself.

I walk down the hall to find Kylie at her desk. She looks up from twisting her purple hair around her finger and waves me over when she hears me coming. "You better hurry up and get out of here before that skank cons you into staying longer."

I let out a frustrated breath and lean against the desk. "Too late. Send her client to my room."

"Seriously?" She questions. "You're that easy, huh?" She grins while reaching for the phone. "I had a feeling that was going to happen so I didn't tell Hailey who her client was. You just keep getting lucky, sweets. I'll call and tell him to come back in."

"Alright," I say while walking away. "Send him on back to my room."

I'm in my room for about three minutes before the door opens up and a handsome guy dressed to impress walks in. He smiles at me before reaching out to shake my hand. "Lynx," he offers. His blue eyes meet mine and capture them.

I smile back at him as he begins to look me up and down. "Riley," I say back. "I'll be taking care of you today. I hope you don't mind."

He offers my hand a little squeeze before releasing it. "I don't mind at all." He reaches for the top button of his black button-down and starts to undo it. "Mind if I get undressed?" He lifts a brow, waiting for my response.

I shake my head, embarrassed, and reach for the door handle. "Oh sorry. Not at all. I'll give you a few minutes."

36

I quickly escape to the hall and give Lynx a few minutes to get undressed and comfortable before I knock on the door in warning and push it open.

Lynx is laying on his stomach, dressed in a tight little pair of black boxer briefs clinging to his small, muscular ass.

"Oh thank goodness," I whisper to myself, glad that he didn't decide to get naked like Cale did. I'm not sure I'd be able to handle that at the moment. Cale had me about to explode from touching his body and I have to admit that I'm still worked up and sexually frustrated.

"What was that," he asks.

I smile down at him as he twists his neck to look at me. "Oh nothing. Sorry." I take a second to take in his body and can't help but compare him to Cale. This man is undoubtedly sexy with his dark, messy hair, and muscular, lean build, yet . . . he doesn't even compare to Cale.

My heart skips a beat at the thought of Cale and it's that moment that I realize I miss him already. I've been trying all day not to think about last night and the fact that I fell asleep in his arms, but seeing this gorgeous man and realizing that he *still* doesn't come close to Cale and the effect his body has on me, makes me realize just how much I truly want Cale. I guess six years hasn't done shit to make my heart forget him. It's pretty sad that I just got out of a two-year relationship, yet it's *Cale* that's on my mind. He's always had that power over me.

ASPEN HAS BEEN TALKING ABOUT her job at the salon and other random things for the last hour, but I haven't been able to stop thinking about Cale and the fact that he's at the bar stripping right now. I didn't really think about it much earlier, but knowing that he's there now, taking his clothes off for tons of women that are probably pawing at his body, has me kind of jealous. I hate that they are there and I'm not. I really *want* to go and see what it's like.

"Let's go to *Walk Of Shame*," I blurt out, cutting Aspen off.

Aspen leans back on the couch and smiles as if she's a bit surprised by my request. "Oh boy. I don't think you can handle it." She shakes her head. "As a matter of fact . . . I *know* you can't handle it. You don't even know the things those boys do with their bodies."

Excitement surges through me at the thought of watching Cale move his body, and now I'm anxious to hurry and get there. "I can handle it. That's where you met Slade, right? If you can survive there, then I'm pretty damn sure I can too."

"Yeah," she says with a laugh. "It was a bumpy ride, that's for damn sure." She stands up from the couch when she hears the shower water turn off. "You should go by yourself. I think I'm going to be busy for the next couple of hours."

Standing up, I give her a surprised look as she starts ushering me toward the door. "How damn rude. You're just going to kick your big sister out like that?"

We both look over to the hallway when Slade appears dripping wet, his waist wrapped in a small towel that leaves little to the imagination.

"Damn," we both say in unison.

Aspen gives me a little shove as Slade smiles at us and runs a hand through his wet hair. "Hell yes I am. You have somewhere to be and I have someone to do. Goodbye."

I wave goodbye to Slade as Aspen shoves me outside and kisses me on the side of the head. "Love you too," I mumble.

"Love you, sis, but you gotta go right now." She hands me my purse. "Slade says hi and bye and hopes to see you soon. Tell Cale we love him. Buh bye."

I roll my eyes and smile when the door closes in my face. As *rude* as this was . . . I want that. I want to want someone like that and for him to want me just as much. I never felt that with Tyler. Yeah, I loved him and he loved me, but we were never desperate for each other and never just *had* to have each other. What I wouldn't give to have that feeling, and if I were to admit it to myself, I sort of felt that way last night when being in Cale's arms. I felt this want and need to be close to him. Sort of like I do now.

I blow out a breath while walking to my car.

Walk Of Shame . . . here I come.

I get hit with a brick of nerves as soon as I pull into the parking lot of *Walk Of Shame* and see how many cars are occupying the lot. It's packed and finding parking won't be easy.

"Holy shit, these women don't play around," I mutter. Grabbing my wallet, I shove my purse under my seat and hop out of my car, pressing the lock behind me.

Just walking in the door of this place is overwhelming. My ears are instantly assaulted with the sound of screaming women and I can barely concentrate as the guy at the door checks my I.D. I keep my eyes on the crowd of loud and crazy women as the guy places my I.D back in my hand and greets the group of women behind me.

The crowd is pretty much shoulder to shoulder and I can barely see what's happening on the stage. That is until Cale jumps down into the crowd and starts grinding his hips to the music while bending some girl over as if he's fucking her.

He's wearing a short pair of red boxer briefs and his muscular body is covered in sweat as he continues to grind behind her, working her nice and good, before thrusting her away with his dick and dropping to the floor as if he's making love to someone below him. He's working his hips so powerfully and with such a perfect rhythm that it takes my breath away just imagining being below him. Now I know what my sister meant by not being able to handle this place. I'll never be able to look at Cale the same now, and I'm pretty positive that there's no way that man is *still* a virgin. I guess I didn't really expect him to be . . .

Holy. Hotness.

CHAPTER SIX

Cale

I SLOW MY RHYTHM AND close my eyes as I picture Riley below me. These women might be imagining me fucking them, but I'm imagining fucking Riley, nice and slow, and taking care of her every fucking need.

I feel hands grab at me and start tugging on my briefs, trying to get me naked. Someone gets my briefs down far enough in the back that my whole ass is hanging out, so I push myself back to my feet, smile at the ladies, and slowly thrust the air, giving them a view of my bare ass flexing.

Right as I'm pulling my briefs back up I look to the left and set my sights on Riley. She's looking at me with wide eyes, appearing slightly uncomfortable and out of place. My body instantly reacts to seeing her and I have to fight against my erection, knowing that these red boxer briefs will do nada to hide what I'm thinking.

Ignoring all the women around me, I walk toward her, letting her know that I see her. The last thing I want is for Riley to feel as if she doesn't belong when she's here to see me. She's the most important woman in this damn room and I'm about to show her that.

When I approach Riley, I wrap my hands into the back of her hair and bury my face into the softness of her neck, pulling her as close to me as humanly possible.

She's stiff at first, but loosens up and grabs my forearms as I run my lips up her neck, grinding my hips against her. I hear her let out a little gasp as my erection presses against her stomach, and that little sound alone is enough to make me want her even more than ever.

"You came to see me," I whisper against her neck. I grab one of her legs and wrap it around my waist as I dig my hips into her. "You're the most beautiful girl in this room, Riley. I promise you that."

Reaching for her other leg, I pick her up and wrap both of her legs around my waist, thrusting my hips into her, nice and slow as if fucking her. My hands grip her ass and I hold her as close to me as I can, grinding her against me.

I look up just as Stone slides a chair in front of me, giving me exactly what I need as if reading my mind. Being careful with Riley, I set her down on the chair and then straddle her lap, wrapping both of my hands into the back of her hair and forcing her to look into my eyes. I'm unsure of what she's thinking, but now is the time to show her what she could have. All she has to do is give me a clue that she wants it just like I do.

Biting my bottom lip, I reach for both of her hands, lightly lacing mine on the backs of hers, before running them slowly down my chest and abs, ensuring she feels every ridge as I grind into her. I lean into her and moan against her ear, showing her just how turned on I am without her doing anything at all.

Her body shivers and she lets out a small moan as well, confirming what I want to know, and letting me see exactly what my body is doing to her. Pleased, I pick her back up and grip her ass as she wraps her legs around me once again.

She leans her head back, getting lost in the moment as my body stills against hers and the song comes to an end.

We stand here for a few moments, holding each other, until finally she lets go and clears her throat, dropping back to her feet. "Told you I've always wanted to see male strippers." She smiles nervously and brushes her hair out of her face. "You should go. The crowd is waiting."

I press my lips to her forehead and offer her a thankful smile, before turning away from her and finishing up the show.

RILEY IS OUTSIDE WAITING BY my truck when I'm done. She looks up from her phone and smiles when she sees me approaching. "Done shaking your junk for the horny women already?"

I walk up to her and kiss her on the forehead, before pulling away and laughing. "Yeah, my junk is tired from all the shaking. It's Stone's turn now."

She lets out a small laugh. "Well, you were great." Her eyes search mine before she speaks again. "Everyone loved you."

"You haven't seen anything yet, Riley." I lean against my truck, beside her. "How was your day?"

"Good," she responds. "I'm just a bit tired and sore."

I look around the parking lot in search of her car. "Did you drive here or take a taxi?"

She pushes a button on her key ring, making it beep, before

holding up her keys. "Drove." She yawns and leans against my truck, looking exhausted. "I was only planning on stopping in for a few minutes, but kinda got sucked in by the action," she teases.

I walk around her and open the passenger door to my truck. "Let's go. We'll get your car tomorrow."

She shakes her head while yawning. "It's fine, Cale. I'll just drive and meet you at your house."

Ignoring her request, I pick her up and set her in my truck, refusing to let her drive in her exhausted condition. "Your car will be fine. You're riding with me."

Smiling, she leans back and buckles her seatbelt. "Yes, master Cale," she quips.

"I like that." I respond with a grin. "Say it again."

Laughing, she smacks my arm and reaches for the door to close it. "Back up before your junk gets stuck in the door."

I bite my bottom lip and back away, watching her in amusement. God, I've missed this woman. Having her here reminds me of why I chose to wait in the first place.

By the time we pull up at my house Riley is practically sleeping in her seat. She slowly straightens and looks out the window while rubbing the back of her neck. "We're here already?" She unbuckles her seatbelt and turns to me as she stretches. "Sorry if I dozed off. I got stuck at work longer than expected. I guess I'm a lot more exhausted than I thought." She rubs her neck again. "And sore. Ouch."

I smile at her and gently touch her bottom lip. "No worries." Hopping out of my truck, I hurry to Riley's side before she has a chance to open the door herself. "You don't have to do shit for the rest of the night. I got you, girl."

She lets out a surprised squeal as I reach in the truck and pick her up, throwing her over my shoulder. "Cale!" She grabs onto my shirt and laughs. "What are you doing?"

I slap her ass and start walking for the door. "Stop squirming. I told you that you don't have to do shit for the rest of the night. Did you think I was joking?"

She places her hands on my ass and pushes up as I walk through the door and shut it behind us. "Well, I didn't think that included walking." She looks up at me, and smiles after I toss her on my bed. "What . . . are you going to undress me for the night too?"

I lift my eyebrows and look her in the eyes as I crawl onto my bed and hover above her. "Yes," I say firmly. "You've been taking care of people your whole life. Let me take care of you tonight."

She swallows as her eyes meet my lips. "Cale . . . you don't have to take care of me. You don't owe—"

I cut her off by pressing my lips to hers, gently but possessively, letting her know how much I want her. I've waited for far too long to kiss her, and there's no way I'm holding back. Tonight . . . she's going to see just how fucking good my tongue can make her feel.

She lets out a moan and grips my shoulders as I run my tongue across her lips, hinting for her to open up for me.

"Cale . . ." She moans again as I press my hips between her legs. "I don't know if we should do this . . ."

I smile against her lips and whisper, "*We* don't have to do any-thing." Running my hands down her sides, I kiss my way down her stomach, stopping above her jeans. "Just let *me* take care of you."

Her eyes search mine for a moment, but she doesn't say a word as I work on taking off her jeans. Slowly, I pull them down her legs, kissing the inside of her thighs on the way down, before tossing her jeans aside and gently nibbling her clit through her thin panties.

She squirms and slams her head back while gripping the blanket in anticipation. "Cale," she breathes heavily. "I don't want to mess things up between us. You should stop . . ."

I slowly pull her panties down while looking her in the eyes. "Don't worry about that. Trust me, Riley. You need this . . . just sit back and enjoy it."

Before she can say anything else, I run my tongue over her clit, before gently sucking it into my mouth. The taste of her against my tongue is almost enough to make me bust my load.

I've wanted to taste Riley for so damn long now. I probably shouldn't be doing this so soon, but I can't help myself. She's just so beautiful and tense. She looks as if she hasn't been pleasured in a long time, and I want her to know how good it can feel to be taken care of, especially by me: her *sweet* Cale.

Riley's hands wrap into my hair as her hips buck upward, begging for more, so that's what I give her.

My tongue explores every last inch of her sweet little pussy, tasting it as if my life depends on it. I work my tongue slow at first, teasing her and making sure that she's left wanting more. Then I speed up, fucking her with my tongue, before slipping my finger into her tight little pussy, pumping in and out as I move back to her clit.

Squeezing her hip, I pull her body closer to me while giving her just a small taste of my skills.

Her grip on my hair tightens as her legs begin to squeeze my face. "Oh God . . . Oh God . . . Cale . . ."

I suck her clit into my mouth, working my tongue and finger fucking her until she's shaking beneath me, her pussy now clenching around my finger. Her muscles tighten so hard that it almost hurts my damn finger.

I look up at her and run my tongue along her folds one more time, before pulling my finger out and sucking her sweet release into my mouth.

Smiling at her new, relaxed state, I crawl above her and press my lips to her forehead. "Goodnight, Riley."

Not wanting to pressure her any more than I have and make her feel uncomfortable, I help her back into her panties before heading for the door on my way to sleep on the couch.

"Goodnight," she whispers softly. "I . . . uh . . . I'll see you in the morning."

I keep my cool until I shut the door behind me. "Fuck me," I growl out.

One taste. One fucking taste and I'm ready to give her all of me. I want to bury myself between her legs so bad, but I know that moving things too fast will only ruin her.

She's too fresh out of a relationship and too concerned about ruining things between us to be able to take that step. Truthfully, I don't even know if she's going to be able to handle what I just did to her. I took it easy on her tonight. Just wait until she can see how rough I can be.

"Shit . . ." I strip down to the nude and lay on the couch, knowing that I won't be sleeping for shit tonight. My dick won't either.

Closing my eyes, I grab my shaft and slowly stroke it to thoughts of Riley riding my hard cock. I want to feel her take it deep and hard, knowing that she's the first to take it.

My strokes become faster as I think back to the sexy little sounds that Riley made when she came on my tongue. "So fucking hot, Riley."

A few minutes later and I'm busting my load all over my tight abs, wishing that it were inside Riley's tight little pussy instead.

Fuck me . . .

CHAPTER SEVEN

Riley

I'VE BEEN LAYING HERE FOR the last hour, unable to shut my mind off and fall asleep. Guilt has been eating at me, making it impossible to shut my eyes.

I should feel guilty for letting another man touch me so soon. I should feel guilty for kissing another man, and enjoying it, but I don't. No . . . I feel guilty for not feeling guilty and knowing that there is only one reason for that: Cale Kinley.

I know without a doubt that if it had been anyone other than Cale I would feel bad for letting another man touch me. Don't get me wrong; I still love Tyler. I mean . . . we were together for two years, so how could I not. I can't just shut my feelings off. Of course I still care about him, wonder what he's doing and how he's feeling now that I'm gone.

The part I don't understand is why when Cale's lips were on me that not one thought of Tyler crossed my mind, as if he was forgotten. Cale consumed my every thought and need, making me feel . . . alive, and cared for. He made me believe for just a small moment that it's possible to let everything go and let someone else take care of you. I really needed that and he could tell. He's always been able to read me.

Now I'm left with another question: how does he feel about me? I know he loves me as a friend and that he'll do anything for me, but would he really go out of his way to please me sexually if his only feelings toward me were platonic? Knowing that he's a stripper confuses me, because I'm sure he doesn't have a problem with sexual attention, and it makes me believe that he possibly does have real feelings for me. Male strippers are known for their reputations. Considering what they do, it's plausible that they're sexually active with probably about seventy percent of the girls that come and see them, but I hope that's not the case with Cale.

Throwing the blanket from my legs, I quietly get out of bed and walk through the living room on my way to the bathroom. I'm sure to be as quiet as possible, worried that I'll wake Cale up. He's had a long night and the last thing I want to do is take away from his sleep.

On the way back to the bedroom, I find myself wanting to see Cale one more time before falling asleep. For some reason my body aches just to get a glimpse of him.

I quietly make my way over to the couch and peek over it.

"What are you doing, Rile?"

I jump back from the sound of Cale's voice. I wasn't expecting him to be awake.

"I couldn't sleep. I just wanted to make sure you were sleeping."

He tiredly smiles at me and reaches for my arms, pulling me onto the couch with him. "I'll help you fall asleep. Come here." He lifts the blanket so that we're both underneath, before snuggling me to his chest and wrapping his arm around me.

I let out a small gasp when I feel his bare dick against the exposed skin of my belly. "You're naked, Cale?"

He just pulls me closer and starts rubbing his hand through my hair, calming me. "Just close your eyes, Rile. I got you." He kisses the top of my hair. "Go to sleep "

I'M JUST FINISHING UP WITH Lynx when I hear the door open behind me. I got a little behind because Lynx constantly wanted to talk and request that I spend extra time on his upper thighs. Every time I tried moving to the next body part, he kept saying that his muscles were still tense.

Feeling frustrated, I don't even bother turning around. "I'm almost done here. Come back in ten please. I apologize."

I hear the door close behind me, so I automatically suspect that the person left, but when Lynx opens his eyes and smiles past me, I realize that the person is still in the room.

I quickly turn around and get ready to usher the person out when my eyes set on Cale. He smiles at me before turning to Lynx. "No wonder your ass wasn't at the club."

Cale lifts an eyebrow as Lynx sits up and slowly gets dressed. "Yeah, well I was feeling a bit tense and this beautiful lady was helping me relax. What's it to you?"

I see Cale's jaw tense, but he quickly shakes it off and leans against the wall as Lynx finishes dressing.

I look between the two of them, before setting my gaze on Lynx. "So I'm guessing you're a stripper too?"

Lynx gives me a cocky grin, before walking up to Cale and

squeezing his shoulder. "Nah . . . I'm the boss man. Right, Cale?" He winks.

Cale shrugs his shoulders and eyes him carefully as he reaches for the door handle. "When you're actually there," he says stiffly.

Lynx brushes off Cale's coldness and turns back to me. "I'll see you in a couple days, Magic hands." He winks and then disappears out into the hall.

Cale grunts to himself and quickly starts getting undressed as I clean and prepare the bed. "Is he in here a lot, Rile?"

I smooth out the new sheet and look behind me. "He's been in here a couple of times. He's pretty persistent when he wants something. I guess I can see why now."

Cale reaches out and grabs my chin, bringing my eyes up to meet his. "Has he tried anything with you? Tell me right now if he has."

I shake my head. "No, Cale. Nothing besides the extra time that he requests on his upper thighs, but I'm starting to get used to that with this job title." I let out a small laugh, but Cale still seems tense.

"Promise me that you'll let me know if he touches you. I don't like the idea of you two in here alone together. He's got quite the reputation at the club."

I place my hand on his arm and he releases my chin. "Don't worry, Cale. I'll be fine." I point down at the bed. "Now get your ass naked so I can get started." I offer him a lighthearted smile. "I'm starting to see that you do everything naked."

He pulls his jeans down and I turn my head away so he can get out of his boxers. "I'm happier when I'm naked, Rile. What can I say?"

I'm happier when you're naked too . . .

When I turn back around, Cale is laying on his back, looking up at the ceiling. The small towel is doing an even shittier job of hiding his junk than the last time.

Squirting some oil into my hands, I start at Cale's shoulders and slowly work my way down his chest. "You working tonight?"

He lets out a small moan when I reach his lower abdomen. "Yeah . . ." he breathes. "In a few hours actually."

The way that he bites his bottom lip each time my hands get lower on his abdomen makes me want to see what he'll do if I touch him sexually. Would he stop me or let me keep going? I try to push the thought aside, but each time I notice him bite his lip and growl I feel my insides jump.

He seems a little tense after seeing Lynx in here . . . He did do me a little favor last night. I just wouldn't be a very good friend if I let him go to work like that, now would I? I'm going to say no . . .

Taking a deep breath, I round the table without removing my hands to create a better angle, and then slide my hands under the towel, wrapping both of them around his thick dick, slowly stroking up and down, feeling it quickly growing in my hands.

"Oh shit . . . Rile." He bites into his lip again, but harder this time, as he grips my waist. "Fuck . . . my cock is so hard for you."

As his grip on my waist gets tighter, my hands work faster and firmer, being sure to pleasure him just as much as he did me last night. His dick is now so hard and big that I definitely need both hands to take care of him.

My heart is racing, but I don't want to stop. Touching him and knowing that I'm giving him pleasure has me more turned on than I've ever been in my entire life. I've waited a long time to touch him like this . . .

"Fuck yes, Rile . . ." He sits up and bites my shoulder, but not hard enough to hurt me. "Keep going. Ah . . . fuck me, Rile."

I lean my neck back as he runs his lips up the side, moaning all the way up until he stops at my ear. "You feel so fucking good, Rile." He moans. "I bet your pussy would feel even better . . ."

I close my eyes from his words and almost feel as if I'm on the verge of having my own orgasm. Stroking his dick, I find that both of us are now moaning, until finally he releases his load on his stomach, before pulling my bottom lip into his mouth and biting it.

As soon as he moans into my mouth once more, I surprisingly find my own release. I instantly feel embarrassed, shocked that something like that could happen without even being touched.

"Shit, Rile." He lies back on the table and runs his hands through his thick, messy hair. "I love it when you touch me."

He looks over at me and grabs my arm as I take a step back. "What's wrong?" He smiles at me and looks down at my legs that are still slightly shaking. "Did you orgasm, Rile?"

I nod my head, my fingertips instantly going to my mouth to create a diversion, too embarrassed to actually speak.

Cale grabs the towel and wipes himself off, before standing up and grabbing my chin after removing my hand from my mouth, forcing me to look up at him. "Well damn, Rile. That's the hottest thing I've ever heard." He smirks down at me and wets his lips. "Knowing that I can make you come without even touching you . . . is by far the sexiest, most satisfying thing that's ever happened to me. All it does is make me want to bend you over this massage table and fuck you until we both can't walk."

"Cale . . ."

He places his finger to my lips and bends down to whisper in my ear. "As soon as I know that you can handle it . . . you *will* be the first woman to have me inside of her. I promise that . . . Rile. Just wait and see."

I stand here, frozen and unable to think clearly as Cale gathers up his clothes and gets dressed.

He must be able to tell that his words have shaken me up, because the next thing I know I feel his lips on the top of my head, before I hear the door open.

"I'll see you tonight, Rile."

Shaking off my frozen state, I turn to Cale and offer him a small smile. "Yeah . . . I'll see you later . . . um . . . after work."

The door closes behind him and I instantly go into panic mode.

"He did not just say that, Riley." I walk over to the bed and start stripping it down, barely able to even function right. "You're just hearing things. There's no way in hell that Cale is still a virgin . . ."

I have no idea how long I've been standing here, dazed and confused, when my door opens and a woman walks in.

Pulling myself together, I smile at her and introduce myself, before walking out into the hall, giving her time to get ready.

How I'm going to be able to function for the rest of the day is beyond me. I had to have heard him wrong . . .

"Yeah, that's it." I try to convince myself. "I'm tired. He could have said anything."

The woman calls my name, interrupting my thoughts, so I shake off my personal thoughts and prepare to make it through the day, hoping that I'm just going crazy.

Cale . . . a virgin . . . me his first . . . friends . . . we're just friends . . .

CHAPTER EIGHT

Cale

MY SHIFT ENDS IN TWENTY minutes and I can't deny that I'm a little disappointed Riley didn't stop in to see me. I haven't heard from her since I left *Sensual Touches* and it's really starting to bother me.

I guess she wasn't ready to hear that I really did wait for her, and I bet that she doesn't believe me. I wouldn't believe me either if the roles were reversed. A virgin stripper. . . . No fucking way. Impossible right? Well, I'm the fucking exception. She is the reason that I'm the exception.

I look up from the ground when I feel a hand on my shoulder. Stone grins like a fool. "Dude . . . you've been standing there for ten damn minutes now. Just get the hell out of here. You're useless here in that state."

Shaking my head I steel my jaw. "Nah, I'm good. Just get the hell back over to your side, man. I don't want your dick over here."

Stone laughs and starts backing up. "At least I'm actually working my dick, bro. That's more than you can say." Grinning like a fool he gives me the middle finger with both hands, before busting back into a dance.

I get my head back into the game for the last ten minutes, trying my best not to think about Riley and whether or not I fucked things up.

Just as I'm pushing through the crowd of women and getting ready to head into the back room, I spot Riley sitting at the bar talking to Sara.

Sara looks over at me and notices the stupid ass grin on my face, raising her brows as she figures it out. Hell yes it makes me happy as hell to see that Riley is here. I don't give a shit who knows.

Gathering up my shit, I get dressed quickly and snatch my tips from Kash, tossing him a pile of twenties on my way out the door.

I stop dead in my tracks when I notice Lynx at the bar talking Riley up. That dick better learn his place when it comes to my woman. She may not know it yet . . . but she's my girl. I'm going to make that very clear, and real soon.

"Just admit that you came to see me," Lynx says with a confident grin that makes me want to choke the life out of him. "I can definitely put on a show one night if it keeps you coming back."

Riley laughs as if she finds him amusing, but doesn't say anything as I approach them at the bar.

Lynx quickly turns to me as I place a kiss on Riley's head and wrap my arms around her from behind. "I didn't think you'd show up," I whisper next to her ear. I look up at Lynx as I say the next part. "I'm glad that you came to see me. I'm ready when you are."

Riley takes one last sip of her drink and slides it across the bar to Sara. "Thank you for the drink, Sara." She gets ready to reach for cash, but Sara and I both stop her.

I look at Sara. "I'll pay for it."

She shakes her head. "It's on me. A little welcome home present. Well besides what I'm sure you've given her." She winks and walks away.

Lynx stands up at the same time that Riley does. "Well, I guess I'll be seeing you tomorrow," he says stiffly. "Same time as the last." He raises his drink to me and smirks. "You did good tonight, Cale. The women got a good show. *All* of them."

I tense my jaw and bite my tongue. I know damn well what he's doing. "Let's go, Rile." I place my hand on the small of her back and guide her outside, fighting the urge to kick the shit out of that dick.

As soon as we reach my truck, I slam Riley against it and crush my lips against hers, claiming them and letting her know how much I want her. Fuck Lynx. He can't have her, not now or ever.

Seeing another man wanting her only makes me want to take it out on her *sexually* and give her all that I have. I may not end up being her first, but I know damn well that I will be her second and her *last*.

Lifting her leg, I thrust my hips into her and moan against her lips. "I want to be inside you so bad, Rile." I kiss her again, before whispering against her lips. "Let me give myself to you. I want you to be my first. I know you may not believe me, but I would never lie to you. You know that. I've done sexual shit, Rile. Lots of things, but I've never entered a woman. I promise you that."

She moans loudly and grips the back of my hair as I suck her bottom lip into my mouth. "Cale . . ." She moans again as I grind my hips between her legs. "You really waited all this time for me?" I roughly kiss her neck and nod my head, just eager to continue tasting her. "What if I told you that I'm still a virgin? Would you still want to make me your first?"

Her words cause my heart to beat erratically in my chest and I freeze mid-kiss. "What?" I pull away and run my hands through my hair. "Are you, Rile? Are you still a virgin?"

She nods her head and covers her face. "I just couldn't do it, Cale." She pushes me away so she can get some air. "Every single time that Tyler and I began to get sexually active I would stop him right before he could enter me." She looks up to meet my eyes. "I kept thinking about you and wondering if you really meant what you said about waiting for me. It didn't feel right so I never had sex with him. I only allowed him to touch me sexually. No wonder he didn't want to follow me to Chicago . . ."

"Holy fuck, Rile." I run my hands through my hair and start pacing. "You telling me that you're a virgin makes me want to fuck you right here, right now." I stop pacing and press Riley back against my truck. "But it also makes me feel like it needs to be special for you, and whenever you're ready. My virginity doesn't mean shit to me as long I lose it to you. It could be in the fucking dirt or mud for all I care."

Riley swallows hard, before standing on the tip of her toes and wrapping her arms around my neck. "Is this really happening right now?" She questions. "I thought that us waiting for each other was just some stupid fantasy that I dreamt up. I thought I was being an idiot."

"Hell no, Rile." I lean down and press my lips against hers. "You really have no idea how much I really care about you, do you?"

She shakes her head and bites her bottom lip.

"Well fuck. I'm going to show you." I open the passenger door and point. "Inside. Now."

With her eyes locked on mine, she climbs into my truck and wraps her legs around me as I step in between them. "I've missed you, Cale." She lets out a small breath. "So much. There were times when I almost ran away in the middle of the night and got on a plane. I had tickets each time, but always talked myself out of it, knowing that I couldn't leave grams like that."

I grip the back of her hair and lightly tug. "Me too, baby. But you're here now and I'm going to make up for it." I bite her bottom lip before releasing it. "Let's go."

AS SOON AS WE PULL out of the parking lot I place her hand on my hard cock, letting her know what she's doing to me, before I slide my hand up her dress. Her pussy is so warm and wet, just waiting for me to touch it. I love that . . . my pussy.

We drive in silence as I gently slide my fingers in and out, loosening her up for what's to come when we get home. Knowing that no man has been inside her has me so anxious to sink deep between those beautiful thighs and take her over and over again, all night long. Now that I know how much she wants it too . . . it's happening.

Once we pull up at my house, I pull my fingers out of her pussy and suck them into my mouth, looking her straight in the eyes. She lets out a small moan and grips the seat. "Riley . . . are you sure you want this?" She nods her head. "You do realize that once I fuck you that it will be happening every day and there's no turning back to just being the old Rile and Cale right? I will pleasure you any and every chance that I get and there's no taking it back: giving me your first time."

"Cale . . ." She reaches for the door handle. "I have always wanted you to be my first. I just didn't think it would actually happen. Knowing that it can. . . . I'm not passing that up for anything."

I feel my chest ache at the thought that we had to go so long without each other, waiting for this fucking moment that should have happened six damn years ago. "Good . . . because I wasn't willing to let you."

Jumping out of the truck, I run over to her side and open the door. I lean inside and wrap both of my hands into the back of her hair, before pulling her toward me and kissing her long and hard. I place one hand on her knee and slide it up her leg, shoving a finger inside of her, while biting her bottom lip and tugging.

"Fuck me . . . I can never get enough of kissing you, Rile. I wanted to kiss you so damn bad the night that you left, but I didn't have the balls to mess things up for us. If I would have kissed you then I know I would have given you so much more that night in the pool, and I couldn't make love to you and just let you leave. I knew I had to wait."

She smiles against my lips. "It's a good thing, because if you would have kissed me . . ." She grips my hair. "Especially like this, then there's no way I would have gotten on that plane. Just one kiss was all I needed from you."

I lean in to kiss her again, but stop when her phone goes off. "Ignore it," I whisper.

"I plan to." She pulls me closer between her legs and reaches her hand down in between us to rub my cock.

I throw my head back and grip her hair tighter, so damn turned on by her touch. "Undo my pants, Rile."

Without hesitation she starts to undo my pants, but her phone goes off again, causing us both to freeze.

"Dammit," she mumbles. "I'm sorry. Let me turn it on silent."

I stand patiently as she pulls out her phone and unlocks the screen to silence it. The pained look on her face tells me who it is and the moment shatters on the spot.

She awkwardly clears her throat and turns her phone on vibrate. "Well that kind of kills the moment. I'm so sorry." Her whole mood has changed and now I feel as if comforting her has become my priority. Riley has a big heart and I'd be stupid not to know how this moment is affecting her.

I pull her chin up and gently kiss her lips. "It's okay, Rile." I rub my thumb over her bottom lip. "Let's go inside and I'll make us a late night snack before bed. "Sound good?"

She nods her head, ashamed, and runs her hands through my hair. "Thank you, Cale. I just want this moment to be the two of us. I don't want any hint of Tyler in the back of my mind."

I kiss her again, letting her know that I'm okay with it. "You can't just shut your feelings off, Rile; I know that and I don't expect it. This won't be our last opportunity. Trust me."

She smiles as I help her out of my truck and guide her to the front door.

I definitely want her mind to be focused on just me once I'm burying myself between her sweet thighs. It will happen soon.

Just not tonight . . . tonight she knows how much I care about her.

CHAPTER NINE
Riley

IT'S BEEN TWO DAYS SINCE I received those missed calls from Tyler and I respect with everything in me that Cale has given me some space in case I wanted to call him back. I thought long and hard about it, and then decided against it. He broke my heart when he decided just *two* days before we were to leave that he didn't want to be a part of the plans. Why should I call him back? He's the one that didn't care enough. He didn't even come to say goodbye the day that I left.

Cale and I are sitting on his couch watching hilarious prank shows and snacking on popcorn, and right now . . . that's all that matters. He's been able to keep a smile on my face throughout the pain that I thought I'd be feeling when I got home, and he's had my back through everything. I'm here and I'm focused on the now.

Tyler is no longer clouding my thoughts and I want Cale to see that.

Setting the bowl of popcorn aside, I straddle Cale's lap and gently kiss him on the lips. His lips are so soft and delicious that I unconsciously lick them before pulling away. I swear that I could kiss him all day and never grow tired of those lips. I've waited too long to not take advantage now.

"Damn, Rile." Cale squeezes my hips before moving down to my thighs, while running his tongue over his lips. "What are you trying to do to me? Are you trying to get me naked, because it won't take much more of that."

I lean my head back and moan as he buries his face into my neck and roughly kisses it, pushing me down onto his lap. "See what you're doing, Rile? You feel that?" I still can't seem to get over feeling his dick against me. It's so damn big and hard . . . and I want it, every inch of it . . . of Cale. My Cale.

He starts grinding below me, rubbing his hardness between my legs. "Yes," I breathe. "God . . . yes . . ." Just the thought of him being inside me makes me break into a sweat. It still amazes me how turned on I get with Cale. It's overwhelming.

After not feeling him touch me for two days, I feel like I could orgasm just from the feel of his tongue alone. That's how good this man is and I have a feeling that he knows it. He may be a virgin . . . but the rest of his body isn't . . . far from it.

"I want to take you somewhere, Rile." He runs his lips up my neck and stops at my ear. "Will you come with me?"

I swallow hard from his words. He just had to use the word *come*. "Cale . . . it's like two in the morning. Isn't it a bit late to take me somewhere?"

He laughs against my neck and squeezes my hips, lifting me from his lap. "It's never too late, Rile." Standing up, he reaches for my hand and pulls me into his chest. His hands tangle in my hair as he runs his tongue up my lips, tasting me. "Fucking delicious, baby."

Smiling, he walks toward the door, picking up his keys on the way out. I follow behind him, curious to where it is that he wants to take me so late at night. I have no clue where he wants to go, but truthfully I'd go anywhere with Cale. I always did in the past, including late night trips . . . but we were just kids then. Sneaking out late at night was in. We're definitely not kids anymore and don't need to sneak out to hang out.

I'm so anxious when we get into Cale's truck that I can't stop looking out the window, trying to figure out where he's taking me. It takes me a good five minutes to figure it out.

"Cale . . ." I sit up straight and look out the window. "Are you taking me to your old house?"

He smirks and pulls off to the side of the road, killing the engine on his truck. "I thought a late night dip sounded good. You know . . . pick up where we left off six years ago."

I sit still as Cale jumps out of the truck and jogs over to my side, opening my door. "But didn't your parents move out like five years ago?"

Laughing, he reaches into the truck and pulls me out, onto my feet. "Yeah, they did." He shuts the door behind me, and then starts pulling me through the grass, toward the back of his old house.

"What?" I look around me, nervous that someone will see us, possibly resulting in cops. "We can't just swim in some stranger's pool, Cale. What if someone catches us?"

He stops and picks me up, wrapping my legs around his waist. As soon as his lips meet mine, all worries seem to disappear. All that exists is Cale and I. Right now I could care less about the consequences.

Walking through the grass, he somehow manages to keep his

lips on mine until we're both sinking into the deep water.

The water is cold at first, a shocker, but as soon as Cale pulls me into his arms . . . he's all that matters. My body is slightly shivering as he swims us toward the side. It reminds me of the last time we were here: the night that I left.

"Remember this?" Cale questions as he holds me up against the side of the pool.

Biting my bottom lip, I nod my head.

"Good . . ." He slides his hand behind my neck and hovers his lips above mine. They're so close that I can almost taste him. "I'm about to do to you what I wanted to do six years ago."

His lips slam against mine, stealing my breath away. I can barely breathe at the moment as I'm taken back to six years ago. I almost feel as if I'm getting the one moment that we missed out on, the moment that I could only dream about *after* I was gone.

"Are you on the pill, Rile?" His eyes meet mine as he pushes my hair out of my face. "Are you?"

I nod my head and rub my thumb over his sexy bottom lip. All I want to do is suck it into my mouth, so I do. I suck it so hard that he growls.

He leans in and kisses me again, hard and firm as he finds my aching pussy with his free hand. I moan against his lips as two of his fingers enter me. They feel so big, but I relax for him and let him loosen me up.

"So good, Rile." He pulls his fingers out and slides my shorts over to the side. I can feel him messing around between our legs, probably pulling himself free from his black pants. He's not wearing any boxers. That was noticeable as soon as he came out of his bedroom earlier, so it doesn't take long before I feel him poking at my entrance.

I shake in Cale's hold, as he looks me in the eyes. I'm so overwhelmed with emotions that I can't even manage to speak. This man has been my best friend for ten years, and I have spent most of those years dreaming of this very moment.

"I've been waiting so long to be inside you, Rile. Are you sure you want this?" He rubs his thumb over my bottom lip as I nod my head. "Say it for me. Tell me that you want me inside you. I want to hear it from your lips. I've waited too long not to."

I lean my head back and moan as I feel the tip of his dick push against my opening. There's no doubt in my mind that I want this. Not having him inside me right now is torture. "I want it, Cale. I've always expected you to be my first." I lean in and whisper against his mouth, "Make love to me."

With those words, he slowly enters me, inch by inch, him holding me so tightly that I can barely breathe.

"Oh fuck," Cale whispers. "You're so tight, Rile. So fucking tight." He slowly pushes all the way in and stills, practically holding me against the wall with his dick. He's breathing so hard right now, that I can feel his chest hammering against mine.

It hurts, but feels so good to have Cale inside of me that I don't want him to stop. He can't. I dig my nails into his arms, letting him know that I need a minute. "It's so big, Cale." I let out a calming breath. "I need a second. Don't move."

Being sure not to hurt me, he reaches back and tugs his shirt off and over his head, before tossing it into the grass. He grips the edge of the pool with one hand and my waist with the other. "Can I move now?"

I wrap both of my arms around his neck and squeeze, preparing myself for him to move. "Yeah," I whisper. "I think I'm okay now."

Pressing his lips against mine, he slowly pulls out and pushes back in, both of us moaning into each other's mouths.

He does this a few more times, as gentle as he can, before his movements pick up, becoming more steady, until he's consistently thrusting inside of me, making me feel so damn good that it's surreal. Having Cale inside of me is so overwhelming that I can barely breathe from the emotions that are taking over me.

Gripping my thigh, he raises it and pushes in hard and deep, before stopping and grinding his hips. He's so deep that I feel as if he's about to rip me apart.

"Cale . . ." I dig my nails into his shoulder as he pulls out and shoves himself in deep again, stopping to kiss me on the lips.

"I want to fuck you so much harder, but I'm holding back, Rile." He lifts me up with his thrust. "Can you handle it harder?"

Hearing him ask me if I can handle it harder sets me off, and suddenly all I can think about is him fucking me so hard that I'm screaming his name. I want him so bad right now. So. Bad.

"Yeah," I say softly. "I can handle it."

"Alright, Rile." He wraps his hands into my hair and tugs. "Don't be afraid to scream. I don't give a shit who hears us. This is our moment . . . just the two of us."

I nod my head and almost feel myself come undone when he digs his teeth into his bottom lip and begins taking me hard and deep.

All I can hear are the sounds of the water slapping between our bodies and our heavy moans. Cale works fast, slowing down once in a while to kiss me and make me feel special . . . and it does. It's as if he knows exactly what he's doing and he's an expert at pleasuring women. He's almost too good to be true, and now the thought of him being inside another woman kills me.

My thoughts cause me to dig my nails into his back roughly, instigating his movements to pick up and become harder.

"This cock is yours, Rile. No one else has had it. Never fucking forget that." He pushes into me and stops. He's breathing heavily, his strong chest moving up and down. "I want to come inside of you, baby."

"Yes . . . yes." I pull him closer to me and kiss his chest. "I want you to."

Gripping my thigh, he pushes in even deeper and rolls his hips. He does this a few more times until I'm practically screaming and shaking in his arms, about to come.

"Yeah, Rile." He pulls out before pushing in deep. "Come for me, baby. I want to feel you squeeze me."

Leaning my head into his neck, I dig my nails into his back as I feel my orgasm taking over. In that moment, Cale thrusts into me a few more times before I feel the pulsations of him filling me with his own orgasm.

Knowing that no other woman has experienced this with Cale has me on some kind of high. He's inside of *me* right now, holding *me* and kissing *me*. A part of me is selfish and wants to keep Cale to myself. I don't want any other woman to experience this side of Cale.

We're both wet and completely satisfied, holding each other tight . . . in someone else's pool.

I would've never thought of my first time being like this, but it was perfect. This pool is where Cale and I spent most of our time in the summer. This pool is where I imagined giving myself to him numerous times. This pool is the last memory I had of him over the last six years.

Now this pool is where we've given ourselves to each other. It's our pool. Our memory to keep and I'll *never* forget his moment. *Ever.*

I feel Cale smile against my neck, before he kisses it and pulls out of me. "Holy shit." Cupping my face, he kisses me long and hard before resting his forehead to mine. "I want to take you again, right here, right now. Is that bad?"

I let out a small laugh and smile. "No," I say breathless. "It's definitely not bad."

He releases my face and pulls his pants back up. "I have a feeling we should get out of here. You were kind of loud." He smiles and I slap his chest.

"Oh . . . just me?"

He laughs and hops out of the pool, pulling me out behind him. He quickly grabs for his shirt and picks me up, throwing me over his shoulder.

He carries me through the grass and over to his truck, the two of us soaking wet and laughing. Setting me down against his truck, he kisses me one last time before opening the door for me, and giving me a boost inside.

When we arrive back at his house, he lets us both in and immediately undresses me as soon as he closes the door behind us, dropping our soaked clothes to the floor.

After we're both completely naked and standing here, he picks me up, wrapping my legs around his waist before carrying me to his bed.

He crawls in behind me and snuggles up against me, covering us up. He notices me shivering, so he pulls me closer to warm me up, just as he always has. "I got you, Rile. I'll always have you."

I smile to myself and grip his arms, feeling completely satisfied and alive, knowing that he does. *He's always had me . . .*

CHAPTER TEN

Cale

I'VE BEEN LAYING HERE FOR the last three hours thinking about tonight. Being inside of Riley was the best feeling in the damn world, and I know without a doubt that no other woman would have been able to make me feel that way. I've always known that and that's why I waited for her.

Fuck having meaningless sex just to experience a bunch of women and get off. None of that matters and I know damn well that it could never feel as good as having sex with someone you have a personal connection with. When you have that, the pleasure is intensified. You feel *everything*.

Watching Riley sleeping in my arms makes me want to bury myself between her thighs and really take her. She's seen my sweet side. I just hope she can handle my dirty side too, because she's about to experience it real soon. I'll let her sleep it off for tonight, because I'm not going to be selfish with her. Riley doesn't deserve that shit.

Pulling Riley as close as I can, I bury my face into the back of her neck and gently kiss her, wanting to show how deeply I care about her.

"Goodnight, Rile," I whisper.

The real pleasure is about to start . . .

SLADE, HEMY AND STONE ARE sitting around like idiots, looking at me as if I've grown a second dick. If it doesn't stop, then I'm going to nut punch the closest one.

"What are you idiots looking at?" I shove a fry in my mouth, eyebrow raised, as I look around the table.

Slade stands up and walks over, sandwich and all, stopping in front of me. "Stand up."

I stand up.

He smirks. "I want to shake your dick and congratulate it on finally becoming a man."

I shove him backward, making him bump into Hemy. "Fuck you." I reach down and adjust my hard dick. Thoughts of Riley naked have been on my mind all morning, leaving me hard, and there's definitely no hiding it. "Talk all you want, assholes."

Stone gets up and starts fucking the edge of the table like an idiot. "Is this how you did it?" He slows down and acts as if he's about to blow his load.

"How the fuck do you idiots even know my business?"

Hemy nods to Slade. "This asshole told me in a text. Ask him."

Slade shrugs his shoulder while biting into his steak sandwich. "Aspen, man. Your girl was on the phone with her for a good hour, talking about how *sweet* and *passionate* it was."

The guys start laughing as if it bothers me. Fuck them. I can't help it that I'm good at making love. "Laugh all you want, because I'm going to make that girl feel so fucking good that all of your women will be complaining to each other and talking shit about how all you guys care about are your own dicks. My woman will be completely satisfied. So fuck you."

"Your woman?" Slade asks with a sly grin. "It's like that already?"

"What . . . are you fucking surprised?" I watch as he walks around the table and takes a seat again. "I wouldn't have waited all this time for a woman if she wasn't worth it, man. Riley is more than worth it, and when she's ready . . . yeah . . . she will be *my* woman."

Stone squeezes my shoulder. "I feel ya though, guy. Sage is the one for me. Being inside her–."

"Fuck you," Hemy shouts. "Say another fucking word and see if I don't shove your dick up your ass. That's my sister, fucker."

"Yeah, I am your sister's fucker," Stone says, egging Hemy on. This dick still has some shit to learn, because that's the last thing you want to do.

Cracking his neck, Hemy stands from his chair and starts walking around me to get to Stone, but I put out my arm stopping him. "Dude, chill. All you fuckers chill and eat your damn food. Can't go anywhere with you dicks anymore."

I feel Hemy's chest flex under my arm, so I pull it away and say fuck it. I'm hungry. These two can kill each other all they want.

Stone stands up and smiles as Hemy approaches him, trying to prove he's badass. "Don't hate me, because I might be your brother-in-law someday. It'll be all good. I promise."

"Hey!" We all look away from the table when Sage comes storming in with Onyx beside her. "Sit down, Hemy! Don't you even think about it."

Hemy gets *the look* from Onyx, so like a good boy he backs off. I don't blame him. Not only does he have a spitfire for a sister, but also his woman is just as wild as her. I don't know how he handles it.

Next thing I know Hemy has his mouth pressed against Onyx's and his hands are groping all of the inappropriate places. I'm pretty sure that's my cue to leave.

Standing up, I pop one last fry into my mouth before tossing some cash on the table. "I'm out. I've gotta go keep my eye on Kash and make sure he can handle his first night on the floor." Walking over, I place a kiss on the side of Onyx and Sage's cheeks, before turning back to the guys. "This kid better not make me work tonight."

I get a, "Get the hell out of here," from Hemy and an "Alright, go fuck off," from Slade, before Stone just waves and grabs his woman.

"What a great group of friends," I mutter to myself. Thank God Riley is back. I don't know how much longer I can handle these assholes.

I'VE BEEN HERE KEEPING MY eye on Kash for the last two hours, and so far I haven't had to save him. I got to give the kid some credit. The women seem to be enjoying themselves.

I have a feeling that he's been watching me a lot, because right now he's got some girl on her knees and he's grinding his dick in her face. The women always seem to love that.

Pulling out my phone, I send Riley a text, hoping that she's not busy. I've been thinking about her all damn day, reminding myself of the moment we shared in the pool. The best damn moment of my life.

Me: How are you doing? Are you at home?

I get a response almost immediately.

Riley: I'm good. I'm not home at the moment.

I stare down at my phone, my stomach sinking from her stiff text. We haven't spoken all day, and I have no idea how she's feeling about last night.

Me: Can I pick you up in an hour?

Riley: No

"Shit." Dropping my phone down onto the couch next to me, I run my hands through my hair. My jaw stiffens as I stand up and get ready to just leave and go find her.

"Because I'm already here."

I turn beside me to see Riley standing there, looking drop dead gorgeous in a little red dress. Her hair is curled and pulled over to her right shoulder, and her lips are slightly tinted pink.

"Fuck me, Rile." I grab her hand and slowly spin her around. "Are you trying to make me take you right here?"

Smiling, she wraps her arms around my neck and steps into my body. "What if I am?"

I slide my hands down her back and stop on her ass, cupping it. "Then you better be ready, because I don't think I can wait another second." I bite her neck, before pulling away. "Especially after seeing you in this dress."

Leaning her head back she laughs. "When did my Cale become so dirty?" Stepping up on her tippy toes, she sucks my bottom lip into her mouth, before releasing it and sliding her hands up the front of my shirt. "I definitely like it. A lot."

"You haven't even begun to see how dirty I can get, but you're definitely pushing me right now." Grabbing her legs, I wrap them around my waist and carry her through the darkened room and to the back corner.

Everyone is too busy paying attention to the new dick that's swinging around on stage than to even notice us. Slamming her up against the wall, I slide her dress up her body. "See the things you make me want to do?" I grind my hips into her and wrap my hand in her hair. "Are you ready for this, Rile?"

She doesn't say anything for a few seconds. She just plays with the ends of my hair and looks me in the eyes. "I've never been more ready for anything, Cale. Trust me."

"Neither have I." Reaching down between us, I work on getting my cock out, while pressing my lips to her neck.

"Hurry, Cale." She tugs on my hair. "I've been thinking about you inside me all day. I need this right now."

Hearing those words set me off. Dropping her feet to the ground, I bend down and yank her panties down her legs, before shoving them in my pocket.

Then, I pick her up and wrap her legs back around my waist, before sliding inside of her. "Oh fuck." We both moan out at the same time.

She's so wet and ready for me that it's hard to not bust my load just from the thought alone. Riley Raines . . . the woman I have wanted for most of my damn life.

I slowly slide in and out, stretching her to accommodate my size, before thrusting into her deep and hard. She lets out a small scream, but muffles it against my chest.

"It's okay, baby." I pull out and thrust into her again, grinding my hips into her as deep as I can. "Let it out. I don't give a shit who hears."

Moaning, she presses her lips to mine as I push into her again. I push into her harder and harder each time, slamming her against the wall with my thrusts.

"Shit, Cale . . ." She digs her nails into the fabric of my shirt and buries her face into my neck. "Oh my God. Yes . . . faster."

Speeding up, I take her as hard and fast as I can, feeling her pussy squeeze around me, bringing me to my own release.

My cock pulses inside of her, filling her with my cum. Biting her bottom lip, I hold her up with my hips and wrap both of my hands into the back of her hair. "Shit, Riley." Both of our bodies are covered in sweat. This place has never made me sweat so fucking much. "You can't dress like that anymore around me. I can't fucking handle it."

She smiles against my lips. "I was hoping for that."

"Cale, dude, what the fuck are you doing back there? Kash needs you for a minute," Lynx yells from across the room. Lazy motherfucker.

Riley's eyes widen and she throws her hand over her face. "Oh. My. God." She starts struggling to get back to her feet. "I almost forgot where we were."

I kiss her one more time and smile against her lips as I readjust myself. "Dude, I'm coming."

She slaps my chest and playfully covers my mouth. "Shh . . . don't say that."

"Well hurry the fuck up."

I press my forehead to hers. "Wait for me." I pull her bottom lip into my mouth. "Let me go help this dick and then we'll leave. Yeah?"

She nods her head and works on pulling her dress down as far as she can. "I'll wait in your truck so I can be panty-less alone."

I reach into my pocket and pull my keys out, handing them to her. "You won't be panty-less and alone for long. Trust me."

Raising a brow, I back up and start walking, before turning around to see what the hell Kash needs me for.

The faster I do the faster I can make it back out to my woman . . .

CHAPTER ELEVEN
Riley

HOLY SHIT! I FALL AGAINST Cale's truck and run my hands over my face. "What the hell was that?" I never act this way. Ever. Cale just does something to me that I can't explain. It's insane and so is what we just did. "Wow . . ."

Anyone could've walked back there and caught us. Then what? He could've lost his job. I would've felt like a complete idiot. I definitely need to get a grip before it's too late.

Unlocking his truck door, I jump inside and rest my head against the back of the seat. My pussy is still pulsing from my orgasm and I can't help but to smile. I shouldn't be smiling after what we just did, but I can't help it. Nothing has ever felt so good in my life. Nothing.

Tyler was never able to give me orgasms. He tried multiple

times and I always had to fake them just to make him happy. It always left me feeling like shit and a complete failure afterwards. Not with Cale. With Cale I almost feel like an idiot for having one too soon. Is that a thing? Shit . . . I don't know.

A few minutes later, the driver's side door opens and Cale jumps inside with a look of aggravation. "That dick head."

I look at him and laugh. "What?"

A small smile crosses Cale's face. "He wanted me to teach him a new dance move. He actually stopped in the middle of his performance so he could ask me to teach him a new move." He shakes his head while starting the engine. "That kid needs some serious work if he wants to make it here."

I can't help but to laugh. His face always cracks me up when he's aggravated. I've always found it hard to take him seriously, probably because his aggravation has never been aimed at me. Thank God.

"He seemed to be doing good to me."

Cale sits up straight and grabs my thigh. "Oh yeah." He runs his hand higher up my thigh and stops right below my pussy. "So that's why you were so wet earlier?"

I squirm as he starts tickling me. "No . . ." I say in between laughs. "No . . . stop it!" I slap at his hand until he finally stops and smiles at me.

"I didn't think so," he says confidently. "I was pretty sure it was all me." He winks and I shake my head at him.

"Confident Cale." I reach over and grab his dick, almost making him swerve off the side of the road. "You do something to me."

"Shit, Rile." He grips the steering wheel, fighting hard to keep his eyes on the road. "What did I turn you into?"

I release his dick and lean back into my seat. "A woman that likes to tease you and see you squirm. You've been doing it to me for years and just didn't know it. You and your little touches. You didn't think that I noticed how close you were to my ass and pussy sometimes? I noticed. Very much so."

Cale smirks. "Well you never said anything." He glances over at me. "I wanted to touch you so bad. That was me getting as close as I could with still being able to control myself. It was harder than you think. Trust me."

My stomach does some kind of little happy dance as I remember the old times with Cale. It's crazy how you can want something so bad and then it happens years down the road. It almost feels as if no time has passed at all.

With Cale . . . I feel like we're still teenagers. He's always made me feel younger than I am. Knowing that I can finally touch him has me all worked up and extremely aroused . . . again.

Reaching for his jeans, I slowly undo them. I tilt my head and look up at Cale to see him watching the road with a smirk. "What are you doing?"

I bite my bottom lip as I pull his erection free, running my hand up the length. "I'm just admiring your body." I sit back in my seat and take in the image of him driving with his dick out. "I definitely like this view."

Cale glances over at me. "Oh yeah?" Keeping his eyes on the road, he grips the steering wheel with one hand and his dick with the other. "What about this?"

A small gasp escapes my lips as he slowly begins to stroke himself. "Oh. My. God." I fan myself off and crack the window some more. "Yes. The view is definitely getting better. Keep going." I whisper the last part, completely lost in him.

Leaning his head back, he quickens his strokes, letting out a small growl. "Do you have any idea how many times I have done this to thoughts of you, Rile?"

My heart jumps out of my chest from his words. "No, I don't."

Feeling completely turned on, I spread my legs a little and moan. "Tell me."

He notices me beginning to squirm in my seat so he lets out a small, amused laugh. "Too many fucking times." He slows his strokes for a second, before he releases his dick and grips my thigh, yanking me toward him. "Almost every damn time you left my house." He pushes my dress up, baring my lower half, and runs his fingers through my slick folds. "Did you ever pleasure yourself while thinking of me . . . huh, Rile?"

I press my head back into the seat and grip it as his finger slips inside of me, slowly pumping in and out.

"Did you ever imagine me fucking you in your bed all those times that I slept in your room?" He shoves his finger in deep and stops. "Did you ever imagine me deep inside you, taking you and making you scream all night? Did you," he whispers.

I jump and grip the seat tighter when he finds my spot. "Yes!" I scream. "Yes . . . so many times. I could never sleep," I admit. "I kept imagining how it would feel."

"Stroke me, Rile." We pull up at a stoplight, but Cale is looking at me as if he could care less what others may see. "Touch me like you always wanted to. I. Want. You. To."

I moan out as his fingers pump into me, fast and hard. "Cale . . . oh my God. That feels . . . so . . . good."

"Touch me," he growls out.

Looking around me, I realize just how dark it is and how high up we are in his truck. It gives me the courage that I need. Reaching over, I take him in my hand, stroking him, and imagining that we're the old Cale and Riley. I'm finally able to touch this man and it feels so damn good.

Leaning toward him, I take him in both hands and pump as fast as I can. Cale has me on the verge of orgasm. "Keep going," I moan. "Faster, Cale."

Turning the corner, Cale slams the truck into park and leans into me, fucking me with his fingers as fast and hard as he can, until I'm squirming in my seat, my arousal covering his fingers.

Not even a few seconds later Cale falls apart beneath my touch, releasing himself onto his shirt. "Fuck me, Rile," he says through heavy breaths. "You've got me feeling like a fucking horny teenage boy again."

I burst into laughter in between heavy breaths. "I hope that's not a bad thing."

Shaking his head, he pulls his shirt off and balls it up, before tossing it in the backseat. "Nothing you do to me can ever be bad, babe."

I feel my heart soar as he flashes me his sweet, dimpled smile. He's the most beautiful man in the world and here I am in his truck. I'm finally able to do the things to him that I've wanted to do for most of my life, and I don't plan on stopping anytime soon.

Shifting the truck into drive, Cale reaches over, intertwining his fingers in mine. "I'm happy that you're back."

"Me too," I say with a smile. "Oh . . . I almost forgot." I shift in my seat so that I can face him. "My parents are having a cookout tomorrow and they want you to come. They've been asking about you. Aspen and Slade will be there too. Are you up for it?"

He smiles while pulling into his driveway. "You know I'm in. I haven't had the chance to bug your parents in a long time; too damn long."

I roll my eyes at just how much my mom loved Cale. I swear she had her own little crush on him. "I'm sure my mom won't mind one bit."

He points to his tight chest and abs. "I'm not sure she can handle all this new goodness that I have. Your father might have to keep her contained."

"Someone's a little cocky." I lean in and motion for him to

meet me half way. "Come here."

Smiling, he leans in and reaches his hand behind my neck. Just as he's about to kiss me, I grab his nipple and twist it. "Mmm . . ." he moans. "Are you trying to work me up again?"

Sucking his bottom lip into my mouth, I slap his chest, before letting my hand trail down it. "A little sleep would be nice . . . so . . ." I bite his bottom lip and pull away. "I think I'll go to bed instead."

He gives me a long, serious look, before jumping out of the truck and running over to my side.

Before I can lock it he pulls my door open and reaches inside, tossing me over his shoulder. "You should know better than to tease me, Rile. Haven't you learned anything about me over the years?"

He shuts the door and slaps my ass, before laying me down into the grass and crawling above me.

Looking into his eyes, I tangle my fingers into the back of his hair. "I don't want this to end, Cale."

He swallows and reaches down to brush my hair out of my face. "No one says it has to."

"But . . ." I stop to collect myself. "What if it ruins us? I can't lose you, Cale."

Pushing my thigh up, he presses himself into me and kisses me long and gentle, before pulling away. "I will never let that happen. I'll die before it does."

Rolling over, he pulls me into his chest and we both lay here, looking up at the night sky just like we used to do some nights after a late night swim at his house. It's so calm and relaxing that I almost feel myself falling asleep, but I keep catching myself, not wanting to lose one minute that I have with Cale.

"It's okay if you fall asleep," Cale whispers. "I'll carry you inside."

I shake my head and wrap my fingers in his. "I'm fine . . ." I yawn. "I'm not going to fall asleep."

"That's what you always say," he says softly.

Next thing I know, I'm falling asleep in his arms . . . just like I always did.

Cale has always been my comfort and safety . . .

CHAPTER TWELVE

Riley

"HURRY UP," I MUTTER UNDER my breath while looking up at the clock on the wall. "Ten more minutes. Ten more minutes."

Mr. Peterson attempts to sit up, but I politely push him back down onto the table. "No more flipping over please, Mr. Peterson. We only have ten minutes left of your session."

Relaxing once again, the elderly man places his hands behind his head and lets out a long sigh. "An hour isn't enough time. What you need to do is teach my damn wife how to do that stuff you do with your hands. That's what I need."

I let out an amused laugh while firmly massaging his left calf, being sure to work out the knot as best as I can. "I'll see what I can do, Mr. Peterson." I smile down at him as he struggles to look up at me. "But then you may not need me if I do that."

"Nonsense," he growls. "You're not getting rid of me that easily. I haven't felt this young in ages. My wife . . ."

Mr. Peterson continues to babble on about his wife, but all I can focus on is the fact that Cale will be here any minute to pick me up. It's only been eight hours, but it feels a hell of a lot longer since I've felt his lips on mine, and it's driving me insane.

As much as I would like some alone time with him before the cookout, we're heading straight over to my parents' to please my mom. She's been asking when he's going to come visit her ever since I walked in the damn house a little over a week ago.

My parents haven't seen Cale in over a year, and I know without a doubt that my mom is going to freak out as soon as he walks in the door. I wouldn't be surprised if she attacks him with kisses.

She's always loved Cale, and when I had to leave to help care for my grandmother it seemed as if it hurt her that I had to leave him behind almost as much as it did me. I cried myself to sleep that night, and my mother watched me with wet eyes, telling me that Cale would still be here when I returned. She was right, even though I didn't believe it at the time.

I shake out of my thoughts in just enough time to see that our time is up. *Thank God!*

"Alright, Mr. Peterson. We're out of time."

Grunting, the old man sits up and stretches as I turn on the sink to wash my hands. "Much better," he says in a raspy voice. "My wife might just be a lucky lady tonight, thanks to you."

"Glad I could help," I say, while trying not to let *that* image ruin my day. "So I'll see you the same time next week?"

I get another grunt and a, "Yes," as he stands up, letting his towel fall to the floor. I'm greeted with the sight of his baggy tight-ie whities, making me instantly turn my head and cover my face. That's definitely not a friendly sight.

"Whoa," I say, taking this as my cue to escape. "I'll just head out and let you finish up. Tell your wife hello for me."

I hear a mutter. "Yeah. Yeah." I quickly dodge out into the hall and shut the door behind me.

"Oh, sweet freedom, how I love you," I say to myself while making my way past Hailey's door and down the short hallway.

As I get closer to the front desk I stop and instantly smile when I notice Cale is waiting inside for me. My heart goes crazy just from the sight of him, and I get this sudden urge to run and jump into his arms. Of course I'm not going to though.

I get ready to start walking, but stop and swallow back my jealousy when I notice Kylie's hand slide across the desk and reach for Cale's arm. From afar it looks as if she's rubbing her fingertips over his muscle.

Cale looks down at her hand on his arm, but doesn't say anything as she leans over the desk in an attempt to get his attention.

Seeing another woman want him in that way feels like getting punched in the gut. Even though he doesn't seem interested, it still gives me a sick feeling in my stomach.

If it's like this here—outside of the strip club—I don't even want to begin to think about what goes on at the club when he's half naked and shaking his goods for drunken, horny women. I've gotten a small glimpse, but I'm sure that's nothing compared to what could happen. I'm not sure what to do with that.

Sucking it up, I walk up beside Cale and get ready to greet him. Without hesitation Cale turns to me and wraps both of his hands into the back of my hair, slamming his lips to mine and pulling me as close as he possibly can.

Talk about taking someone's breath away. His lips assault mine, repeatedly sucking and tasting me in a way that almost feels desperate. He's devouring me. Pulling away, he runs his tongue over his bottom lip before biting it. "Shit, I've been waiting all day to do that."

Kylie looks us both over before rolling her eyes and sitting down in her chair, clearly aware that Cale is not interested now. "Looks like I did someone a favor last week," she says stiffly. "Better you than Hailey, I suppose."

Her words somehow piss me off. He's been my Cale for far longer than this girl even knew he existed. Leaning over the desk, I get ready to say something, but Cale pulls me to him, cutting me off.

"Nah, actually you did me a favor." He slaps the desk, before leaning in and sucking my bottom lip into his mouth. "And it's always been her. Simple as that." With a lift of his eyebrow, he grabs my hand to get me walking. "Ready?"

Trying to fight my grin, I nod my head and wrap my arm around his waist as he starts walking toward the door. "So damn ready."

Just as we're about to walk out the door Hailey appears next to the desk, glaring at Kylie and complaining about something. I hear Cale's name, but choose to ignore it. I don't need anything dragging me down at the moment; especially two girls that I can barely even stand to be around.

After hopping into Cale's truck I reach for my seatbelt and get ready to pull it down, but look up surprised when Cale reaches over me and reclines my seat back as far as it will go.

"What are you doing?" I laugh as he crawls over the seat until he's hovering over me, gripping the seat with his hand to keep balance. I can't help but to notice the way his muscles flex as he stares down at me.

"Something I've always wanted to do in the past." He positions himself between my legs and presses his lips to mine . . . hard; so hard that it almost hurts. "I've always wanted to take you in my truck," he says against my lips.

"Cale . . ." I run my hands up his strong back as he sucks my bottom lip into his mouth, teasing me and turning me on completely. "There's people everywhere," I say with a small moan.

He grips my thigh and smiles against my mouth. "Then let them watch." His lips slam against mine, causing me to moan out as my eyes close. "Fuck, I can't hold back with you, Rile. I've kept my hands off of you for long enough; too damn long. Touching you everywhere is the only thing I can think about anymore."

I start reaching for the back of his shirt, getting completely lost in the moment, but jump when I look beside us to see Slade leaning against the truck, casually just chilling and enjoying the show. "Holy shit," I laugh. "Seriously?"

"What?" Cale stops kissing my neck and looks up. "Fucking idiot," he growls as soon as he sees Slade. With his jaw steeled, he rolls down the window, glaring at Slade the whole time, as if he wants to kill him. "What dude? What are you doing here?"

Slade lifts an eyebrow and uncrosses his arms. "Just enjoying the show, man. Don't stop on my account. I'm curious to see just what I need to teach you. You gotta catch up with the big boys now."

Cale's grip on the seat tightens. "You're an idiot," he growls. "What do you really want?"

Slade shrugs his shoulders and grips the window. "Aspen told me you were stopping to pick up Riley on the way over. I was driving by and noticed your damn truck. The windows looked a little frosted and shit, so I came to hurry your ass up."

Grinning, Cale gives Slade the middle finger while rolling up the window. He leans in and kisses me quickly, breathing heavily against my lips. "Dammit! Let's go before this dude busts a nut outside of my truck. Anything can work him up."

I laugh and roll the window back down as Cale crawls over to his seat and adjusts the crotch of his jeans. "Hey, Slade," I say with a small laugh.

Slade gives me a slick head nod and smiles. "Looking good, Riley." Leaning in the truck, Slade kisses the side of my head while smiling over at Cale. "Both of you hurry your asses up."

Cale starts the engine, gripping the wheel while glaring at Slade. "Don't push it, fucker. We're on the way."

Slade winks and turns on his heels, walking over to his nice new car.

"Remind me to kill Slade later," Cale says while pulling out of the lot.

I can't help but to laugh at the boys for acting so silly. I definitely won't mind this kind of entertainment to get us through dinner. "Sure thing," I say with a smile.

I try to stay cool on the way to my parents' house, but the way Cale is rubbing my leg has me squirming in my seat and gripping the seat. The satisfied smirk on his face only shows me that he's doing this on purpose and enjoying this much more than I am.

"You're enjoying this, aren't you?" I grab his hand and place it on his own lap as he pulls up in front of the house. "It's already going to be hard enough to act normal around my parents, pretending as if nothing is going on. Please don't make it harder." I suck in a breath and attempt to compose myself.

He unbuckles his seatbelt and reaches over to undo mine, hovering his lips above mine. "Who said anything about acting normal?" He brushes his lips over mine, causing my heart to jump out of my chest. "You can touch me, kiss me . . . or fuck me for all I care. There's plenty of rooms to choose from." He whispers the last part before smiling and jumping out of the truck, leaving me wanting him even more.

"Damn you, Cale. You're still a pain in my ass," I say to myself while gripping the door handle and jumping out to catch up with him. "Well, it's definitely going to be easy to talk to my parents now," I tease. "So thanks for that image."

CALE

Without bothering to knock Cale opens the screen door and lets himself in, holding the door open for me. My mom is standing in the kitchen mixing some kind of dessert when we walk in. It smells like chocolate. Cale loves chocolate.

"Oooh. Oooh." My mom cleans the chocolate off of her hands hurriedly, and smiles as Cale walks over to her with open arms.

"Did you miss me?" Cale asks while squeezing my mom in a bear hug and shaking her back and forth.

She pulls away and grabs his face, looking him over. Her smile is so big that it looks like her face is going to split open. "You know I did. Look at you," she squeals. "Oh my goodness." She backs away and looks him up and down, taking in his large build. "You have gotten so much bigger since the last time I saw you, Cale, and more handsome too. Oh my. Come here."

She grabs my arm and pulls me next to her, while holding onto Cale's waist. "It's so good seeing you two hanging out again. It makes me feel young again. Isn't this something?"

Rolling my eyes, I kiss my mom on the cheek and laugh. "Yeah . . . yeah. Where's Aspen and Slade?"

My mom releases her grip on both of us and points to the back door. "They're outside with your father."

"It smells so good in here," Cale says before kissing my mom on the cheek. "I've missed your cooking. Don't be surprised if I eat all that dessert you're working on."

My mom blushes while going back to stirring her dessert. "Yeah, well what can I say? That's why I made so much. I learned my lesson eight years ago." She turns to me and winks. "The food is on the grill and should be ready to eat soon. Just hang out for a bit and keep your father company. We all know he doesn't get it very often."

"Alright, Mom. Let me know if you need help."

My mom shakes her head and motions toward the door. "Nope. Just go and enjoy yourselves. Scoot."

Cale places his hand on my lower back and guides me toward the sliding door. "Your ass looks fucking delicious in those shorts," he whispers, before sliding the door open and pulling me outside. "Can't wait to taste you later."

I break into an instant sweat from his words mixed with the heat. As soon as my dad sees us, he waves us over, holding up a beer for Cale. I just need to get away from this man before I melt into a damn puddle at his feet. He's the perfect distraction.

Pulling away from Cale, I rush over to Aspen and sit down in the chair next to her while Cale goes to hang out with my dad and Slade.

My dad stands up as soon as Cale approaches. Handing him a beer, he grips Cale's shoulder and greets him with a smile. I'm actually surprised to see how happy my dad looks to see him. I knew he always liked Cale. He just didn't want to admit how much.

I turn to Aspen. "This is torture," I say in a hurry.

Aspen takes a sip of her pop and looks over at the picnic table where the guys are hanging out. "Tell me about it. I'm bored already. Mom talked our leg off when we walked in the door and dad keeps talking about his work."

I shake my head and look in Cale's direction to see his tight muscles flexing as he grips his beer and laughs along with the guys. "No, I meant Cale. All I want to do is take him up to my old room and jump on him. It's like I can't even be in the same room without touching him. You know?"

Aspen smiles at my comment and lifts a brow as she watches the guys. "I definitely know, sister. Welcome to my world."

We sit here, just watching the boys for a few minutes, before Aspen speaks up, breaking the silence. "So what *are* you and Cale anyway? Are you doing this whole 'friends with benefits' thing? Or what? That could definitely get messy, so be careful."

I let out a frustrated breath and grab for Aspen's pop, taking a quick drink. My mouth suddenly feels extremely dry. "I don't know, Aspen. I care about Cale a lot, you know that, but I really don't know what he wants out of this. I'm worried if I ask him that I'll mess up what we have. I can't have that. We've been friends for too long, so I'm just sitting back and enjoying the ride."

"Literally," Aspen replies.

"Shut up," I say, while punching her in the thigh. "Can you talk any louder?"

"Ouch, asshole." Aspen smiles, taking another sip of her pop. "Nothing to be ashamed of."

We both look up when my father calls us. "Girls. Get over here and eat."

We both grumble to each other before getting up and joining everyone else at the table. I take a spot next to Cale as Aspen takes her place beside Slade.

Dinner passes quickly as my parents talk to Cale about what he's been up to over the years. Leaving out the male stripper part, Cale tells them stories from his bartending experience. Now I'm just hoping they don't look up *Walk Of Shame* and decide to drop in for a quick drink sometime. They are supportive like that and it might be a little awkward to explain.

After all conversation with my parents is done and everything is cleaned up, we decide to head inside for a few drinks and a game of darts. The boys talked shit to each other the whole time during dinner, betting money on who would win. Everyone was pretty surprised when my mother jumped up and threw in some money on Cale. That definitely gave him an extra confidence boost, not that he needed one.

There's fifty bucks on the line, so the boys are getting into a serious mode, trying to intimidate each other while us girls sit back and watch.

My parents are sitting in the next room watching a movie, just enjoying the fact that we're all still here. It's not very often that they have both of their girls home, and they're definitely working to keep us here as long as they can.

I have to admit that we're all having fun, a lot more fun than I expected. It sort of feels like old times, back when Aspen and I lived at home. I like this carefree feeling right now, and I'm not ready for it to end anytime soon.

"You lucky, shit," Slade spits out while yanking the darts out of the board. "That was luck not skill, so stop that smiling bullshit."

Cale tilts back his bottle of beer and grins even bigger, clearly enjoying this. "Oh trust me, that was all skill, bro." He holds up his free hand, showing it off. "My hand is talented as fuck, Slade."

"Nah . . ." Slade throws his first dart, hitting the bull's eye. "That's skill. Might as well give me your dick shaking tips now."

Ignoring Slade, Cale walks over to me and wraps his hands into the back of my hair, pulling me in for a kiss. His lips are soft and sweet, tasting of the chocolate dessert that he recently ate. "I can't wait to get you alone. As soon as I win this asshole's money, I'm taking you to the nearest bed and letting you have your way with me." He smiles against my lips when I grab his ass and squeeze.

"Oh, is that right?" I run my hands up his strong back and dig my nails into his shoulders. "So I can do anything that I want?"

He pulls my bottom lip into his mouth and nibbles it. "Anything," he breathes. "You're the only one with that power, so I would abuse it if I were you."

Cale clenches his jaw when one of Slade's darts comes flying at his head. "Seriously?"

Aspen wraps her arm around Slade's neck and pulls him down to her level so that she can kiss him and whisper something to him.

"You both want to play now, huh?" I grab one of Cale's darts and throw it at them. "I think us girls should get in on this game. Double it."

We're all standing here bickering, trying to decide on what to do when the doorbell rings.

A few minutes later, my mom walks in and takes one look at me in Cale's arms, before clearing her throat and looking around awkwardly. "Riley . . . Tyler is at the door. He said he's here to talk to you."

I just about pass out when Tyler steps into the room, looking at me as if he's waited forever to see me again.

His blonde hair is cut short and slightly messy, and he's dressed in a pair of old jeans and a white shirt. I almost forgot just how cute he is, and seeing him standing here . . . for me . . . makes my heart sink.

Holy. Fucking. Shit.

CHAPTER THIRTEEN
Cale

FUCK ME. . . . MY EYES MEET Riley's and I can see her being emotionally pulled in different directions, about to lose her composure. This is not good. Not good for me at all.

Knowing that he's here to win Riley back makes me fucking sick. Now that I know what he looks like, it's easier to picture him putting his hands all over her and I don't like it. Not one bit. In fact . . . it makes me hate him.

"Tyler . . ." Riley places her hand over her mouth in shock, looking him up and down as if she doesn't know whether to slap him or run to him. "What are you doing here?"

Tyler swallows and looks around the room. Riley is standing close enough to me that I'm sure there's reason for him to question our intentions. "I miss you." He looks at me as he says the next part. "I need to talk to you, Riley. Can we talk in private?"

Everything in me is screaming for her to say no, but I know Riley. I know her more than anything, so I already know her answer before she says it.

"Uh . . . yeah." She looks around the room and stops when her eyes land on me. "I'm sorry. I need a few minutes."

I place my hand on her hip and give it a small squeeze, before nodding my head and turning away. I can't stand to watch her walk away with him. I can't fucking do it.

"Well fuck," Slade says after they walk away. "Just keep your cool, man."

I grip the pool table until my knuckles turn white. "I'm cool, man." I feel Aspen's hand on my shoulder. "I'm good, Aspen. I'm good."

It feels like a lifetime has passed since she's been alone with him talking. I know for a fact that me being here is making it harder for her. I hate that feeling. I hate feeling like I'm the *other* guy.

After about twenty minutes, I can't take it anymore. I feel like I'm about to burst into that room and rip his fucking head off. I keep imagining different scenarios, replaying over and over in my head, and that's when I realize that I need to get out of here before I do something I'll regret later.

"I need to leave," I grind out. Pushing away from the pool table, I turn around and give Slade and Aspen one last look. "I'm about to lose it."

Slade grips my shoulder, but I shake it off and rush out of the room before he can try to stop me. Slowing down for a quick minute, I smile when I reach the living room where Riley's parents are watching a movie. "Thank you so much for dinner."

Kay stands up and kisses my cheek. "Promise me you'll come back soon." I get ready to pull away, but she squeezes my arm, stopping me. "Promise me, Cale," she says firmly. "You know Riley more than anyone. You remember that."

Nodding my head, I pull away and give my respects to her father before hurrying out the door and to my truck. As soon as I close the door behind me, I slam my fist into the dashboard until it's covered in blood. Why the hell does this feeling kill me so much? Why do I want to kill this man?

"Fuck me," I growl.

I may give her a day to get her head on straight, but there's no way in hell I'm giving up and letting him have her back. Riley is mine. She has been from the very first day we met.

It's time that I show her that . . .

WE'VE BEEN STANDING HERE FOR almost twenty minutes, yet Tyler hasn't said a word. He always does this when he's upset and trying to think of the best way to start the conversation.

"Tyler, just talk." I take a seat on the foot of my bed and look up at him. "What are you doing here? We broke up. Remember?"

He runs his hands over his face before looking at me. "I know, Riley, but damn. I've missed you so much." Looking me in the eyes, he walks over to stand in front of me and reaches out for my hands. "I've been going crazy without you. You haven't answered any of my calls and it's been killing me. Killing me, Riley."

I swallow back the guilt and pain that his words bring and try to keep in mind that *he's* the one that decided to break it off at the last minute. *He's* the one that said it would be better to just be friends.

"I'm sorry, Tyler, but I needed time. I can't allow myself to just sit around and mope over you. I have friends and family here that want to spend time with me and I needed to keep a clear head for that."

"I see that," he says stiffly. "Looks like you've been enjoying your *friend* out there quite a bit."

Looking away, I run my hands through my hair and swallow. I never meant to be intimate with someone, and especially so quickly after the breakup, but Cale is an exception. He deserves my time and attention more than anyone I know.

"Look, Tyler. Cale has been my friend for over ten years. I never meant for things to turn into something more, but . . ."

Tyler bends down and places his thumb to my lips, shutting me up. "I don't care about that. What I care about is making you mine again." He points down at the floor. "I'm here. I have enough bags packed to stay for a week. If we can make it work then I will fly back home and pack up all of my shit if I can't get you to come back home with me." He leans in to kiss my lips, but I turn my head. "Riley, I still love you. I've given you two years of my life."

His words cause my chest to ache. He's right. Two years means something. Maybe just throwing it away is a shitty thing to do. I'm so damn confused right now and all I want to do is scream.

"Do you still love me, Riley?" He grabs my chin to make me look at him when I don't respond. "Answer me, Riley. You can't tell me that you don't have any love left for me after just a short time of being apart. Tell me the truth."

I hesitate before answering him, because I don't want to give him too much hope, especially when I'm this confused. "Tyler . . ."

"Just give me a yes or no. I don't want an explanation of buts or maybes. Just a simple yes or no."

"Of course I do, but—."

"That's all I want to hear, and that should be good enough to at least try while I'm here." Standing up, he pulls me to my feet. "Tell me that I've got a chance, Riley. Please."

I feel my heart beating out of my chest as I think about Cale and what he must be thinking right now. I don't want to think about me without Cale, but Tyler flew all the way here from Mexico. That has to mean something too. I don't want to be a shitty person to the people that care about me.

I can't do this right now. I can't think straight. My breathing picks up and it's getting harder and harder to breathe. "I need time. I need to get out of here." I begin backing out of the room. "I'm sorry, Tyler."

Turning around, I rush out of the room and down the stairs, gripping the railing a little too tight. My chest feels extremely tight as I make my through the house.

My parents both look up at me as I rush to the game room. My heart stops when I poke my head inside to see only Slade and Aspen.

"He's gone," Slade says stiffly.

My throat burns when I hear those two words. "He left?" I whisper, mainly to myself. I stand there frozen for a moment, before rushing outside. Cale's truck is gone and my heart feels completely shattered.

What the hell do I do?

I want to scream, but instead I walk. I just keep walking, needing to get away from everyone and everything. This is so messed up right now and I have no idea what I'm going to do to fix this. My heart aches for Cale, but my head is telling me that I need to at least give Tyler a chance after coming all this way. I hate this so much.

In the end . . . someone always gets hurt. I just hate that I have to be the one to do it.

CHAPTER FOURTEEN

Cale

IT'S BEEN TWO DAYS SINCE I've talked to Riley and I'm on the verge of losing my shit. She called me a few times the night that I left her parents' house, but I forced myself not to answer it. I want her back, but I want to give her time to get her head on straight first.

The thought that she's possibly been spending time with Tyler has been killing me, but a real man will hurt for the woman he fucking loves.

He's had two days now to prove his fucking point. Now it's my turn, and you better believe that I'm going to give her all that I have. The thought of another man pleasing her will never cross her mind. All she will be able to see is the two of us together.

I snap out of my thoughts when Hemy comes into the room

shirtless, looking for me. "The show is about to start, man. You ready or what," he asks while throwing on a fresh shirt. "Get your shit together."

I let out a frustrated breath and slam back my beer. "Yeah, man. Let's do this shit. Where are Stone and Kash?"

"They're coming out of the other room." Hemy pulls his long hair into a man bun as *Earned It* by The Weeknd starts playing from the speaker. "Fuck yeah."

He pushes the door open and dances his way out first, before I follow behind him a few seconds later, followed by Stone, and then Kash from their rooms.

All at the same time, we find a girl in the crowd and pull her chair to the center, before straddling her chair and grinding our hips.

I made sure to pick someone that I've never met so that I won't give off the wrong idea. It just so happens to be a cute brunette that reminds me of Riley with her big, beautiful eyes.

It distracts me for a moment, but I manage to not skip a beat, moving right into the next move. Tilting her chair back until her back is almost to the floor, I walk over her until my cock is in her face, before I grind my hips as if fucking her mouth nice and slow.

I feel the girl's hands grip onto my ass and squeeze, but I don't let it distract me. I can't. I need to stay in the moment as much as I can.

Maneuvering my way off of her face, I put her chair back into sitting position and make my way up to the stage, meeting the guys in the middle.

We all drop down to the ground, gripping our jeans in the front and pulling as if undressing ourselves, while thrusting in a slow, torturous rhythm. Every girl in the room starts screaming and whistling, wishing that they could be the ones below us. The simple fact that we could have *any* girl in this room used to get me hard, but not tonight, not even a slight chub.

Instead, it gives me a sick feeling in my stomach, reminding me that the one and only girl I want might be with another man right now. The thought causes me to work my hips hard and aggressively, while biting down on my lip to ease my anger.

Keeping balance with one hand, I reach behind me, pulling the back of my jeans down until my full ass is on display. Then, I replace my other hand and grind the stage, giving all of the screaming women a full view of what my ass looks like while fucking.

I can feel the sweat drip down my body with each movement, but that only makes it seem more like fucking, giving the women the image that they come here for.

Standing up, we all reach for our shirts and slowly rip them off, before rubbing them over our cocks and throwing them out into the crowd. A bunch of hands fly up, fighting to get to them first. I almost die when I see Riley walk to the front of the crowd, holding my shirt in her hands.

Her eyes meet mine and pull me in, making it hard for me to concentrate on the rest of the dance. All I can think about is the fact that she's here . . . at *Walk Of Shame*.

Running my hands down my body, I look her in the eyes, biting my bottom lip as I shove my hand down the front of my jeans and thrust the air. Watching the way she looks at me has me running my hand over my slightly hard cock, imagining it was hers instead.

I can see the lust in her eyes, making it very clear that she's been thinking about me over the last couple of days. That pleases me. That means she most likely hasn't been sexual with that prick.

The end of the song is coming, so in rhythm we all turn away from the stage and drop our jeans, cupping our packages with both hands, before turning back around and kicking our jeans off the stage.

The women go crazy, practically fighting each other to climb onto the stage. I look out into the crowd, searching for Riley as we make our way off the stage, but she's lost in the pile of screaming bodies.

Hands grab at us, groping and slapping our asses until we dodge into the back room. I go from seeing the woman of my damn dreams to being closed off in a room with three naked assholes.

Opening my locker, I reach for a pair of fresh jeans and a shirt and quickly get dressed, while the other guys start bickering about who did the best.

"Where the hell are you rushing off to," Hemy asks, while pulling up a pair of jeans.

"Riley's here," I say stiffly. "I'm going to find her."

Lynx walks in with a handful of cash, but I brush past him, not giving a shit about getting paid. I just want to get to my girl before she leaves.

As soon as I walk back out into the club, a few girls walk over and start rubbing their hands on me, saying sexual things, but I don't listen to a thing they're saying. Instead, I push their hands away and look over their heads for Riley.

I spot Riley across the room, slamming back a shot by the bar. Setting her empty glass down, she tosses money in front of her before heading toward the door, dodging out as if she couldn't escape soon enough.

Rushing through the crowd, I run to the door and shove it open, trying to catch Riley before she can drive off. By the time I make it outside, she's already shutting the door to her car.

Running my hands through my hair, I let out a frustrated breath and walk over to knock on her window.

She looks up from the steering wheel, surprised to see me standing outside.

Looking me in the eyes, she rolls down her window and releases a breath. "Cale . . . what are you doing?"

Reaching through the window, I rub my thumb over her bottom lip. "Trying to catch you." I breathe. "Where are you going?"

She looks away for a second, before turning back to face me. "I don't know. I just . . . I just need to get away, Cale. I'm so lost right now. I can't stop thinking about you and what goes on here. It's driving me fucking crazy, but I also have Tyler trying to prove to me that two years isn't worth throwing away. I can't breathe, dammit."

I wrap both of my hands into the back of her hair and lean inside the window. "Here," I whisper. "Let me help you with that." Wetting my lips, I press them against hers, showing her just how much I have missed her.

I feel her breath escape her as she wraps one of her arms around my neck and breaks our kiss. "Cale . . ." she says while fighting to catch her breath. "Are you trying to kill me?"

Smiling, I open her car door and reach for her hand. "Come with me, Rile." She gets ready to say something, but I cut her off. "Please don't say no to me."

She looks at me for a second, before pulling her key out of the ignition and letting me help her to her feet. "You know that always works on me," she says defeated. "Not fair, jerk."

I grin, knowing that she's right. "I know. Now let's go."

About ten minutes later, we pull up in my driveway, parking in front of the garage, and she follows me outside to stand by my side of the truck. She's staring at me as if trying to figure me out.

If she wants to know what it is that I want or that I'm thinking, then I'll tell her. I'm not afraid to.

"I want to fuck you, Rile." Stepping up to her, I grip her ass in my hands and run my lips up her neck. "I want to be deep inside you right now, making you scream my name and forget about that asshole. Is that what you want to hear? I'll always tell you what's on my mind if you just ask me."

Leaning her head back, she lets out a soft moan. "I don't know if that's a good idea, Cale. I'm already confused enough as it is."

Gripping her thighs, I pick her up, wrapping her legs around my waist. "Then let me make it less confusing." I brush my lips under her ear and whisper, "Let me show you what I have to offer you. This can be yours. I can be yours. Every. Fucking. Day."

As soon as her body trembles in my arms, I know that I have her, at least for the moment, and I'm going to consume her in a way that no other man will even come close to.

Riley will see the things my body can do that no one else can . . .

CHAPTER FIFTEEN
Riley

I PROBABLY SHOULDN'T BE HERE right now, but I couldn't fight it. My chest has been aching since the moment I realized that Cale walked out of the door the other night.

I went to *Walk Of Shame* just to watch him from the crowd, just to get a small glimpse of him, but seeing him up there on stage and knowing that every girl in the room was most likely thinking about him fucking them was messing with my mental state even more. I couldn't make myself leave. I had to stay until the end.

I was just supposed to leave after that. I was supposed to drive home and be alone in my thoughts, but instead I'm here . . . with Cale. No matter what was going on in the past, just like now, I've always ended up with Cale instead of being alone. He's always been capable of drawing me to him and making me spend my time with him. The problem is, he's even better at it now.

Gripping him as tightly as I can, I feel a moan escape me as his soft lips brush right under my ear. There's no denying how much I want him right now, and I know he can feel it too.

"Has Tyler been inside you, Rile?" Gripping my ass, he presses me against the side of his truck, causing me to moan out.

Of course not, I want to scream out. We haven't even hung out yet, although I did promise him at least one dinner. I plan to talk to Cale about it before I leave tonight. I just hope that he will understand why I have to do it . . .

I shake my head. "No, but we need to talk . . ."

"Not right now," Cale says sternly. "We have all night. Right now . . . I need you."

I DON'T HESITATE BEFORE SETTING her down with her back pressed against my truck. Her dress rides up in the front, exposing her pink panties, and all I can think about is ripping them off with my teeth. This woman makes me want go fucking wild.

She watches me with lust in her eyes as I pull my t-shirt off and toss it over the truck, good and ready to have her hands all over me. I wasn't lying when I said I want her right now. I. Want. Her. Right. Now. I grip the bottom of her dress and wrap it in my hand, pulling her to me. I can't hold back anymore and I'm hoping she can handle it. "Fuck, Riley," I breathe against her neck. "I want to take you right here. I want to fuck you everywhere."

She lets out a gasp and reaches for the button of my jeans, clearly wanting me as much as I want her. "I really want you too, Cale. I have no idea what I'm doing right now, but I know I've been thinking about this for the last two days." Her fingers work fast on undoing my jeans, while biting her bottom lip. "It's almost crazy how much I want you right now."

I look down at her, my chest heaving up and down as I grip her neck and make her look me in the eyes. "You can have me anytime and anywhere that you please. Not having you touch me is what's driving me fucking crazy." I press my erection against her stomach and she grips it with her hand, running her slim fingers along my length. "Right now I just need you to forget about him. It's just you and me, Rile."

Her breath comes out ragged as her eyes lower to land on my rock hard cock. Her eyes fill with a want that I've never seen from her, and I know for a fact that Tyler will never see that look from her. I'll make sure of it.

She swallows hard, bringing her eyes back up to meet mine. "I don't want to think about Tyler right now. I'm not. I won't. You're all I've been able to think about."

I bite into my bottom lip, before picking her up and setting her on the bed of my truck. "That's all I fucking need right now."

Her legs willfully spread as I slowly pull her dress up, exposing her delicious body that is just dying to be licked and tasted by me.

I grip her hips with force and pull her down to the edge of the truck bed, so her ass is barely hanging on the surface. Then, I bend down and run my tongue up the length of her inner thigh, stopping right by her panty line. "Mmm . . ." I moan against her flesh.

I can tell by the soft moan coming from her lips that my mouth being so close to her pussy is driving her mad. That only seems to make me harder. Moaning, I pull her panties aside and run my tongue over her wet pussy, causing her to grip my arms and squirm. One taste and I'm ready to take her right this second.

I close my teeth around her delicious thigh, giving it a playful bite before pulling away and working my mouth up her belly, my hands pulling her dress up on the way. When the dress reaches her head, I pull it off and throw it into the back of the truck.

With urgency, I position my face between her spread legs again, biting her clit through the thin fabric of her panties. During mid moan, I grip her thong in both hands, ripping each side open, surprising her.

Her legs tremble as she runs her hands over my chest and throws her head back. "I still can't believe we're doing this," she says softly. "People might still be awake."

A soft rumble comes from my throat as I quirk an eyebrow and grip both of her wrists in my hand, pulling her up to meet my abdomen. "Take my jeans all the way off, Rile." I grip the back of her neck and suck her bottom lip into my mouth. "Forget about everyone else."

She slides my jeans all the way down to my knees, looking me in the eyes the whole time. The look in her eyes somehow makes me want her even more. I feel like a beast about to lose control.

I yank her legs, pulling her towards me so my cock is resting above her belly. With one hand gripping her neck, I pull her hips up to meet my stiffness, gently sinking into her heat. I slowly thrust in and out a few times, loosening her up to make room, before giving her my full on thrust that is sure to make us being here known to the neighbors.

She screams out while wrapping her legs around my waist, causing me to thrust harder, rolling my hips in and out, giving her the pleasure that she deserves.

Her hold on my bicep hardens as I grip the back of her neck, wrapping my fingers in her hair and pounding into her with as much force as I can. Being inside her feels so damn good that I almost lose it, releasing myself inside of her right then.

Without pulling out, I grip both of her hips and flip her over so her ass is facing me. I reach down with one hand and rub my finger over her wet clit while pounding into her with fast, consistent thrusts, tugging her hair with my free hand. "Scream for me, Rile. Let it out," I demand.

She lets out a low scream as I slow my pace and wrap my arm around her waist, pulling her up so my chest is pressed against her back. "I don't want to get caught, Cale. Your neighbors . . ."

I bend down so my lips are hovering over her ear before I whisper, "Fuck my neighbors. It's you I want to please."

Locking my eyes with hers as she turns her head to look at me, I pound into her, causing her to scream out this time. She screams so loud that she covers her own mouth, too afraid to be seen or heard.

I quicken my pace while moving my fingers up and down her wetness, knowing that at any moment she's about to clamp around my cock and release her juices. I want to feel it surrounding me and covering me.

With one last thrust, she screams and her legs begin to shake as she struggles to not fall over. "Cale . . . Cale . . . Oh shit . . ."

I support her body with mine and pause for a second, allowing her body to clamp around me as she shakes. "That's it, baby." I kiss her neck and hold her until she's done shaking below me, then, I grip her hips, pull out, and slam back into her.

I do this a few more times, holding her as close to me as possible, before wrapping an arm around her neck as I release myself as deep into her still throbbing pussy as I can. We both let out a satisfied moan as I twist her neck closer and press my lips to hers. "You're so beautiful," I whisper against her lips.

She smiles and hides her blushing face as I pull out of her and clean her off with my shirt.

We're both silent as I climb into the back of my truck and lay down, pulling her onto my chest.

We lay here for what seems like hours, before I finally break the silence.

"Remember laying in the back of my truck outside your house late at night?"

She laughs and wraps her arm tighter around me. "Of course I remember. I lived for those nights, Cale. Do you realize how many times I wanted to crawl into your arms just like I am now?"

Smiling like a fool, I grip her tighter and run a hand through her hair. "I wish you would have, Rile. I definitely wouldn't have pushed you away."

"Good to know," she says with a laugh.

We go back to laying in silence, just staring at the night sky. It's so damn peaceful that I never want to move from this spot.

"Cale . . ."

I press my lips to her forehead. "What's up?"

She hesitates, clearly afraid of my reaction. I can tell by the way she's breathing so heavily.

"Say it, Rile," I say gently. "I never want you to hold back from me."

She sits up and searches for her dress, quickly pulling it back on, making sure that she's covered up. "I promised Tyler that I would let him take me out on a date." She lets out a small breath and repositions herself to get comfortable. "I had to after him coming so far. It just didn't seem right to deny him that small request." She looks up at me, focusing on my lips for a brief moment, before meeting my eyes. "Are you mad?"

Inside I feel like I'm fucking dying. The last thing I want to think about is another man taking her out on a date when I haven't even had the chance. I fucking hate it, but I'm trying my best to not be selfish when it comes to Riley. If she needs to do this, then I need to let her.

"No," I admit. "I'm not mad. I'm jealous as shit and not wanting to share you with another man." I pull her back to me and gently kiss her. "One date. I don't think I can handle more than that without wanting to kill him."

"I think I should go home for the night, Cale." She runs her fingers into the back of my hair. "I'm going out with Tyler tomorrow. It won't be right if I stay here."

I swallow back my anger as my chest tightens in pain. As much as I don't want this, I know that nothing with us will be able to move forward until he's out of the picture. Then, I'm going to make her all fucking mine and hold onto her until I take my last breath. That's a promise.

"I'll drop you off." I hop out of the truck and grab Riley's hand, helping her out and on her feet. "Let's go."

This hurts like a bitch, but there's no way I'm giving up on her. Fuck that . . .

CHAPTER SIXTEEN

Riley

GETTING DRESSED AND READY TO go out to dinner with Tyler is stirring a ton of emotions inside of me. Just a couple of weeks ago it was me and Tyler, and now it's me and Cale, with Tyler fighting his way back into my life. It makes everything a lot more complicated than I hoped it would be. I always thought if Cale and I were to end up together that it would be easy and nothing else in the world would matter, but right now . . . it feels far from easy.

"Riley," my mom screams from downstairs. "Tyler's here. Are you ready?"

Sighing, I grab my purse and slip the strap over my shoulder, before making my way to the stairs. I look down at my mom and shrug my shoulders. "Yeah, I suppose so. I just want to get this dinner over with."

My mom watches me with concern as I slowly make my way down the stairs, passing her without another word. I just have so much on my mind right now that it's making it hard to think straight.

Here I am going out with Tyler while Cale is at *Walk Of Shame*, taking his clothes off for a bunch of horny women. He could have any one of them. Why would he want to wait around for me . . . again?

"Are you okay," my dad asks, snapping me out of my thoughts.

I look up at him and smile. "I'm good. I'm fine. Just tired." *Not really, but . . .* 'I'll be home later. I don't plan on staying out too late."

"Alright, honey," Mom says to my back as I'm walking to the door. "I'll wait up for you. I have a feeling we're going to have a lot to talk about when you get home."

I look over my shoulder at her. "I guess we'll see."

When I open the screen door I look up to see Tyler leaning against his rental car. He's too busy messing around on his phone to notice me approaching. It's probably a good thing, because right now it seems extremely hard to hide the disappointment of what I have to do tonight. One look at my face and it's a given.

I take a second to compose myself before stopping in front of him and clearing my throat.

Tyler looks up from his phone and quickly shoves it in his pocket to show me his full attention. Smiling, he says, "You look really nice." He reaches for the end of my favorite shirt and fingers it. "I've missed seeing this old thing."

I smile small, appreciative of his compliment, before pulling away a bit. "Thanks."

We both stand here in an awkward silence before Tyler holds up his keys and dangles them. "I guess we should get going. We'll discuss the restaurant on the road. Sound good?"

I nod my head and reach for the door handle. "Sounds like a plan."

As soon as I shut the door behind me, my heart starts racing at the realization that this isn't Cale's truck. This is another man's vehicle. My ex's to be more specific; the man that I slept next to for two years. It feels so wrong being here with him and every bit of my body is telling me this.

I sit stiffly, lost in my thoughts as Tyler hops in and shuts his door. Without any warning he reaches over and grabs my hand, pulling it into his lap like old times.

My first instinct is to pull away from him. It doesn't feel right. Not like it used to. "No," I say softly. "We're not a couple anymore, Tyler. Please no touching."

His face registers hurt, but he just nods his head and agrees. "Understandable. Sorry, it just comes so natural with you. I don't want to do anything to make you uncomfortable. No more touching unless you ask."

Relief washes through me that he understands the boundaries of this dinner. The thought of him touching me or trying to kiss me has been eating at me ever since I agreed to this dinner with him. I don't need anything else making me feel more guilty and confused than I already do.

"I know where we can eat at." I sit up and point down the street and over to the left side of the road. "I haven't been there since I was a kid."

Tyler looks over to where I'm pointing and pulls into the left lane. "I'm down."

The only reason I haven't been there since I was a kid is because Cale hates the place. We had one bad experience with some douche giving me a hard time and Cale decided that he never wanted to go back. It reminded him of that issue and always made him want to punch something.

I'd rather take Tyler here to eat dinner than a place that Cale and I enjoy together. It somehow makes me feel a little better about this whole thing.

We don't say much more as we head inside and find an empty booth to sit down in. The waitress nods at us as we take our seats, so we both just reach for a menu from the back of the table and skim over the choices while waiting.

After a few minutes, Tyler sets his menu down and stares at me. I can feel his eyes on me, distracting me from the menu.

"Just say it, Tyler. . . . You know I hate it when you just stare at me like that."

I set my menu down and look him in the eyes. He searches my face in silence before speaking.

"How could you do it?"

We both look up at the waitress as she walks over to take our order. We quickly give her our food and drink order as she jots it down then disappears, leaving us alone in what I'm sure is going to be an uncomfortable conversation.

"What?" I ask, feeling a bit uncomfortable. "What are you getting at?"

His facial expression changes and he suddenly looks angry. "Have sex with that Cale guy."

I suck in a deep breath and bite my tongue. I don't like him questioning me like this, and that look on his face makes me want to slap it off of him.

"Why would you ask me that?" I stop talking and smile up at the waitress as she drops off our drinks, then wait for her to walk away before talking again. "I don't think this is something we should talk about, Tyler."

He reaches for his cup and takes a long, desperate drink. "Oh . . . it's definitely something we should talk about, and your response just confirms my suspicions. Why would you sleep with him? We were together for two years; two years, Riley, and you wouldn't let me make love to you. You've been *here* for less than three weeks and you decide to let that loser in your bed."

Sitting up, I slap the table defensively and get closer to his face, letting him see the anger in my eyes. "I don't want to *ever* hear you call Cale a loser again." I grind my jaw, trying to hold myself back from screaming. "Cale has been in my life a lot longer than you have, and he's always been there for me. You don't even know him, so don't you dare judge him."

The conversation comes to a halt again when our plates are set down in front of us. I'm so angry right now that I almost let my mouth run, not caring that someone else is listening to our conversation. No one gets to talk shit about Cale without getting an earful from me. This man has been everything to me for as long as I can remember.

The waitress smiles at us and tells us to enjoy, before walking away.

I shove my fork into my food and start eating as fast as I can. The faster I eat, the faster I can get this stupid dinner over with. I don't know what he expected to accomplish out of this dinner, but I hope he didn't expect to win me back, because this definitely isn't working.

"Calm down, Riley." Tyler reaches over the table and grabs my fork out of my hand. "Talk to me for a minute. I'm not trying to piss you off. I just want answers. You don't think this hurts me? I'm hurt right now. This hurts me."

I lean back in my seat and take a few breaths to calm myself. "I don't want to fight, okay, but if you keep running your mouth and saying things about Cale then I'm going to leave and never speak to you again. He doesn't deserve you bad-mouthing him when he has done nothing but take care of me."

Tyler's jaw flexes, as he looks me over. I can tell that he's fighting really hard not to tell me how he feels about my words.

"Let's forget about this *guy* for a minute then and talk about us. What about us? Are you really willing to just throw two years away as if it meant nothing to you?"

I sit up and let out a humorous laugh. I can't believe he's going there right now. "Oh . . . I don't know, Tyler. I was wondering the same thing when you decided to back out of our relationship right when we were supposed to get on a damn plane. Apparently our two years together didn't mean shit to you, so why should it mean anything to me now? Tell me!"

Tyler stands up and rushes over to my side of the table, scooting his way onto my bench. "I made a mistake. A huge mistake." He reaches for my face, but I turn away from him. "Riley. Please look at me. I love you. I'm in love with you. After you left, it made me realize how much of an idiot I was for not going with you. I'm here now and we can be together."

I shake my head and run my hands over my face. I don't want to be hearing this right now. I've waited for what seems like forever to hear him tell me he loves me again, and now . . . now here he is at the worst possible time ever and it doesn't mean anything to me.

"I don't want to hear that now, Tyler. I'm sorry, but I'm over what we had. This dinner and conversation are confirming that for me. I don't feel anything. I'm so sorry. I want to be with Cale. I always have."

Tyler stands up and starts pacing in front of the booth. "He's a fucking stripper, Riley." He narrows his eyes at me when I give him a surprised look. "Yeah, I've done my research on your little boyfriend. Is that what you really want? Huh?" He sits back down, but on his side of the table. "A man that takes off his clothes for other women and then comes home horny and ready for you? How do you know what he does at that club? What makes you think that he's not getting off on these women touching him? Open your eyes, Riley. He could have any of those women, all of the ass he wants. He'll *never* be faithful to you and you're stupid if you think he will be."

My heart stops and anger that I've never felt before takes over. Standing up, I walk over to stand in front of him. "Fuck you!" Unable to stop myself, I slap him across the cheek and storm out of the restaurant, needing to get away from him before I break down.

As soon as I'm about a block away from the parking lot, I break down and lose it. My chest aches and I can barely catch my breath. As much as I hate to admit it . . . Tyler's words had an effect on me.

I don't want to think about Cale with other women. I don't want to believe what Tyler said, but what if it's true? What if more goes on at that club than I know?

The thoughts running through my head make me just want to scream. It hurts so damn bad just thinking about Cale possibly wanting one of those girls. I hate it. I fucking hate it.

I hate it, but I love Cale. I've been in love with him for longer than I was willing to admit. There's no hiding it now. This man is going to ruin me . . .

CHAPTER SEVENTEEN
Cale

THE GIRLS HAVE BEEN EXTRA grabby tonight and I can't wait to just get the hell out of here. Here I am . . . with all these women pulling at me and touching me, and *all* I can think about is the fact that *my* woman is out with another man. We might not have a title, but I know without a doubt that she is mine.

No one can make her feel the way that I do for the simple fact that no other man can love her and care for her as much as I do. Actions speak louder than words, and my actions will always be to take care of Riley and *show* her how much she means to me. This Tyler guy needs to hit the fucking road and realize that she's taken. He lost his chance, and these women need to watch their damn hands before I lose it.

The song playing over the speakers slows down, so gripping

my hair I roll my hips, slowing down my rhythm to match the music. *Wicked Games* by The Weeknd is playing, so every girl in this room is hanging on my every move, just wanting me to fuck them to this song later. I can see it in their eyes and it makes me feel fucking guilty.

I don't know what made me think that Riley would be okay with this lifestyle, but the more I'm here, the more I worry that she will start pulling away from me when she sees just how bad it truly can get here. Tonight is one of those nights that would probably push Riley over the edge. Lynx seems to be pushing it to get as dirty as fucking possible.

Doing as Lynx instructed, I strip out of my briefs and cover as much of my cock as possible with my free hand, before replacing my hand with my boxer briefs. Dropping to the ground, I hold the thin fabric over my dick and start grinding on the ground as if fucking someone, long and deep. I feel one of the guys pour water over me, soaking me and making it even harder to cover myself with my white briefs.

I can feel hands grab and slap at my ass as I continue to thrust in a slow rhythm, waiting for this fucking song to end. Every woman in this room now knows what my naked ass looks like while fucking. I don't feel comfortable knowing that Riley should be the only one to witness this dirty moment.

As the song comes to an end I grind my hips one more time, before making my way to my feet. A slim brunette with huge tits instantly plasters herself to the front of my body and grabs my cock. Her other hand reaches around my back side and grips my ass as she starts sliding her hand over my shaft.

"Stop," I growl out, while gripping her wrist and pulling her hand away.

Throwing herself at me, she ignores my demand and grabs at my fucking dick again. "Mmm . . . someone's packing," she slurs.

"Show us your dick, baby, and I'll let you put it anywhere."

I grip her wrist a little tighter this time and get in her face, showing her that I'm not interested. "I'm not going to *fuck* you so just stop."

Pushing past her, I look up just in time to see Riley looking at me from the across the room. I can see the shock and hurt on her face and all I want to do is scream for her to come to me so I can make her feel better.

She shakes her head and starts backing away as I begin making my way through the crowd. I get just a glimpse of Lynx walking her away before a group of girls walk in front of me, blocking my line of vision.

My skin heats up in anger at just the thought of Lynx being with her, so I don't think twice before brushing the group of drunken women off and pushing through them.

By the time I get to where Riley and Lynx are, over by the door, I stop dead in my fucking tracks when I see Lynx pinning her against the door in between his arms. He's whispering something in her ear, but it looks as if she just wants to leave.

Without even giving it a second thought I grip Lynx's shoulder and spin him around, swinging my right fist into his mouth.

"What the fuck!" Lynx screams out in shock. "Did you seriously just fucking hit me, you crazy asshole?"

Keeping my eyes on him, I reach down for my boxer briefs that are now on the ground and quickly slide them back on, before walking over to Riley and grabbing her chin. "Are you okay?" I grip the back of her hair and look her in the eyes. "Did he touch you?"

I feel someone grab my shoulder. I turn around defensively to see that it's only Stone. "You got this, bro?" He asks, while looking back and forth between me and Lynx.

"I'm good, man." I shake his hand off my shoulder and give Riley my full attention. "Did he touch you? Tell me."

She shakes her head and pushes me away, looking hurt and more confused than I've ever seen her. "No . . . but it looks as if *everyone* gets to touch you, Cale."

She pushes me away again, so I back up a bit, giving her space. I never want to make her feel uncomfortable, but I want nothing more than to touch her right now. It leaves me in a fucked up situation.

"Rile, I'm fucking sorry." I grip my hair and growl out in anger at the fact that she had to witness some other girl touch me like that. "I don't want that shit, trust me, but please don't walk out on me without talking to me. You've never just walked out on me. Don't start now."

I feel my heart fucking get ripped out of my chest when I notice that her face is wet. She's been crying. She's been fucking crying while I've been here taking off my clothes for other women and fulfilling their damn fantasies. I'm a dick.

"I'm sorry, Cale, but I can't . . . I just can't." She starts walking toward the door. I grab her arm to stop her, but she pulls it away and gives me a dirty look. That's how I know she needs time alone. "I need to leave right now. Please just understand that. This is so much more than I thought. So much . . . worse."

"I'm sorry," is all I can say. I reach out and rub my thumb over her lip, but she backs away and looks around the room as the women start screaming for Stone.

"I can't handle this, Cale. I thought I could, but I can't. I need time to think." Without another word she rushes out the door, leaving me on the verge of going crazy. I want nothing more than to go after her, but I respect her more than anyone in this world, and if she needs time then I can't take that away from her. I know that and I hate myself for it.

"Fuck!" I slam my fist into the wall repeatedly while yelling out a string of cuss words. "What did you say to her?" I bark at

Lynx as his eyes size me up.

He smirks with a confidence that makes me want to fuck him up even more. "Just told her how it truly is here. How dirty all the women get. The truth. That's what."

"Fucking, piece of shit." I start walking to the back to get my shit and Lynx instantly follows me, talking shit the whole way.

"You're lucky I don't fire your ass for that shit. I don't know who the fuck you think you are."

I ignore him, knowing that if I say anything I'm probably going to break his pretty little face.

Bursting through the door of the locker room, I start pulling out my shit to get dressed.

"Can you fucking hear me, asshole? One more mistake and you're gone. You're lucky that you've been here for as long as you have and that you bring me money, you sorry son of a bitch, or else you'd be so done."

I take a few seconds to breathe and calm down after I pull my shirt over my head. This asshole is lucky that I have a lot of willpower.

"I'm fucking bleeding and it's all because I was talking to that bitch that wants nothing to do with either of us. That's fucked up . . ."

Turning around, I swing out, knocking his ass on the ground. "I fucking quit."

Stepping over him, I rush outside and to my truck. I get in, gripping the wheel for dear life. All I can think about is Riley possibly running to Tyler for comfort, and it's all I need to lose it.

"Fuck! Fuck! Fuck!"

Time . . . how the hell can I give her time when that's the one thing that could possibly make me lose her? Well double fuck . . .

CHAPTER EIGHTEEN

Cale

IT'S BEEN THREE DAYS. THREE damn days and Riley hasn't responded to any of my messages. I feel like I'm going crazy. Riley has never gone this long without responding to me. I've tried giving her time, but I just can't wait anymore. I need to make a move before I lose her completely. I can't let that happen and I won't.

I called her work yesterday and booked every single appointment that she had available today. I've been sitting here in the parking lot on Slade's motorcycle, waiting for them to open. I didn't want her to know I was showing up and I knew that if she noticed my truck in the parking lot that there was a chance she'd freak out and leave.

She isn't due in for another thirty minutes, but I already told Kylie that I'm waiting in her damn room until she gets here, and I don't give a shit what anyone says.

A few cars pull into the lot, so I look down at my phone to check the time. They opened a few minutes ago.

Hopping off of Slade's bike, I set the helmet on the seat and rush over to the door, walking inside. Kylie looks up from her desk and smiles when she notices that it's me.

"Hey, stud," she says sweetly. "Are you sure you don't want to keep me company until *she* gets here?"

I walk past her, ignoring her completely. I don't have time for her shit. I don't want her shit. All I want is to show Riley how much I love her. She may be pissed to see me at first, but I don't care. I have to do this.

About five minutes before Riley is due to arrive, I strip out of my jeans and shirt, before getting comfortable on my back. I was in so much of a hurry that I didn't even bother throwing on any boxer briefs. It's not like I'd be wearing them for long anyways. I plan on spending most of my day, here, naked.

My heart speeds up when I hear the sound of the door opening. I've been fucking dying to be close to Riley, and knowing that she's about to be in the same room is making it very difficult to not just pull her down onto the table and take care of her.

I can hear her shuffling around and getting ready. I'm watching her, but she hasn't even bothered to look at the table yet. She's so damn beautiful that it causes my chest to ache. All I want to do is wrap my hands into that brown hair and pull her lips to mine.

"Good morning," she mumbles. "My name is Riley and . . ." Her words trail off when she finally looks to see who her client is. "Cale," she says in almost a whisper. "What are you doing here?"

Sitting up, I grab her arm before she can walk away. I can see the confusion and hurt written all over her face, and I know without a doubt that she wants to run away and not face me right now.

"Come here, baby." Throwing my legs off the side of the

table, I pull her between my legs and wrap them around her so she will listen to me. "Just hear me out, Rile. Please."

She swallows hard and closes her eyes as I wrap my hands into the back of her hair. "Cale . . . I'm scared. I'm so fucking scared when it comes to you."

"Shh . . ." I gently kiss her neck, enjoying the sweet scent of her skin. Nothing else will ever feel this way and I know that. Now I just need to show her. "I'll never hurt you, Riley. Ever. I want you to know that. Haven't I always been good to you?"

I kiss her neck again, causing her to moan out. "Yes," she whispers. "But if you ever hurt me, it would kill me. Do you get that, Cale? That's why I can't do this. I can't get too deep and allow that to happen."

Running my lips up her neck, I stop below her ear and whisper, "I'll never let that happen, Rile." I suck her earlobe into my mouth and nibble it. "Do you know why?"

She lets out a small breath and shakes her head. "No . . ."

I press my lips against her ear and tug at her hair, getting as close to her as possible. "Because I'm in love with you," I whisper. "I always have been, Rile. I fucking love you."

She lets out a small gasp and presses her hand over her mouth. Pulling away, I look her in the eyes and repeat myself. "I'm in love with you. I will always put you first. I will always make you happy and think of you before anyone else. That is a promise." I pull her forehead to mine. "Do you understand that?"

She doesn't respond, so I ask her again. "Do you?"

"Cale, I can't ask you to do that. I can't . . ."

"You don't have to," I say honestly. "I've been doing it since we were kids. It comes natural to me now. Not doing it wouldn't feel right to me. I quit my fucking job, Rile. I'm going to focus on you." I place her hand on my chest. "This body will only be touched by you. I can promise you that on my life."

I cup her face and run my thumbs over her wet cheeks. "None of that matters to me. This is me showing you how much I love you. Words don't mean shit unless you have the actions to back it up. This is me doing my part. This is me showing you that I fucking love you."

A half laugh, half sob escapes her throat as she rubs her hand over my chest, taking me all in.

The silence in the room is making my heart work overtime. I need her to speak. I need to hear that she's willing to be mine.

"Talk to me, Rile. Please say something."

She reaches her hand up and wraps it into the back of my hair like she always does. Then, her eyes lock with mine, causing my chest to ache in anticipation. "I'm in love with you too, Cale. God, I love you so much that it hurts."

I pull her onto the table with me and crush my lips to hers, just wanting to taste her and feel her against me. "I love you, baby," I whisper against her lips. "I'm your man for as long as you will have me. Only yours."

"Show me," she says with a smirk.

I suck her bottom lip into my mouth and bite it. "Oh trust me . . . I plan to. All fucking day."

She laughs as if she doesn't believe me. "I do have other clients booked today, Cale."

I raise my brows and slide her hand down to my rock hard cock. "Not for the next five hours." I turn us, laying her down on the bed to hover above her. "I'm a greedy asshole today and didn't want to share you for longer than I had to." I smile against her lips. "Fuck everyone else. You're mine until then."

She grips my neck and pulls me down to kiss her, long and hard. "I fucking love you so much."

"Fuck I love hearing that," I growl. Letting my excitement take over, I yank her dress up and over her head, before pulling her panties down her legs and tossing them aside. I need to be inside my woman right now, and I need to show her how much I love her.

Laying her back down from removing her clothes, I get down, in between her legs, and allow my tongue to trail up the inside of her thigh, slowly tasting her. I can already see her juices dripping and all I want to do is lick her clean, tasting her on my tongue. She smells so damn sweet, and I can only imagine her pussy tastes even sweeter right now, just waiting for me.

Grabbing her thighs, I push her legs toward her breasts. "Fuck, I've been waiting for days to do this, Rile." I slowly trail my tongue up the wetness of her pussy, torturing her clit with the tip of my tongue, before slipping my tongue deep inside, getting a better taste. She moans and her whole body shakes with pleasure as I spread her moistness to her clit and slip a finger into her tight little pussy; my tight little pussy.

I swirl my tongue around before sucking her clit into my mouth, being sure to be gentle with her. I suck and lick while moving my finger in and out in a slow, consistent motion, never losing rhythm. I know how much rhythm means to a woman's sexual needs and I will be fucked if I don't give her the greatest pleasure she's ever known. Tyler can fuck off. He's never made her come like I'm about to.

It doesn't take long before I can feel her already starting to clamp down around my finger. It doesn't surprise me though. If I'm good at one thing, it's definitely using my tongue, and I've saved my best for her. I slowly run my tongue in between her lips before sucking them into my mouth and then her clit. When I feel her starting to clamp again, I run my tongue over her thigh, before softly biting down on it. "Come for me, baby," I whisper. "Don't worry about anyone hearing you."

Her body jerks as she clamps around my finger and screams out softly. It's so fucking tight that it almost hurts my finger. It reminds me that I've been the only one to be inside of her.

Right as she's coming, I pull my finger out, replacing it with my tongue. I want to taste her when she comes. "Fuck yeah, Rile." Her breathing comes out in heavy bursts as she continues to scream and moan below me. "Cale . . . Cale . . ." She runs her hands through her hair before biting her bottom lip and looking up to meet my eyes. "Make love to me. Please . . ."

Snaking my arm around her waist, I move up to press my body between her wet thighs. I kiss her, wanting to taste every fucking inch of her. Her lips are the best tasting thing in the world to me, and I swear that I will never be able to get enough.

She moans and leans her head back, pressing it into the massage bed. I love seeing her come undone below me, knowing that I will be the only one. She had her chances and didn't take them. It only makes me love her more.

Gripping her thigh, I slip inside of her, causing her to moan out and dig her nails into my back. "I've missed you inside of me, Cale."

"Say it again," I whisper against her lips.

She leans up and sucks my lip into her mouth, turning me on even more. "I've. Missed. You. Inside. Of. Me." She wraps her legs around my waist and squeezes me hard. "You are my best friend, the man that I love. You and only you."

Her words set me off and before I know it, I'm grinding my hips in and out of her, taking her slow and deep, deeper than I've ever taken her.

With each thrust her nails dig deeper and harder into my flesh, her moans becoming louder in my ear. Something about this moment feels so different than all of the other times we've had sex. Everything seems so much more real.

Maybe it's the fact that I know she loves me now, and this is me proving to her that I love her too. This is us making love.

My hand slips under her neck to grip her hair as I press my lips to hers and continue to make love to her, knowing that this moment is special to both of us. This is the moment that I make my best friend so much more: my woman. This moment I have been waiting on for far too fucking long.

Knowing how this feels, I would wait all over again if I had to. This is a feeling that many men aren't lucky enough to ever experience and I wouldn't give it up for anything . . .

AFTER TALKING AND MAKING LOVE for about the fifth time, I help Riley get dressed before getting dressed myself, then pull her into my arms and press my lips to her forehead.

"Come home tonight, baby," I whisper. "Let me take you out on a real date."

Smiling, she grabs my face and looks me in the eyes. "You making me dinner and taking care of me would be the realest that a date could ever get. If you ask me, you're the only one that has taken me on a *real* date."

My heart swells from her words and a sense of pride swarms through me. "This is why I love you so much, Rile."

Pressing my lips to hers, I kiss her long and hard, not wanting to say bye for the next three hours. I just want her home and in my bed. "Hurry home so I can make you dinner and make love to you all fucking night. I have a lot of making up to do. I'll never again lose time with you."

She smiles and pushes me away as someone knocks on the door. "Okay," she laughs. "I'll hurry back. I promise."

"Home," I say, correcting her.

She kisses me once more and smiles. "Home. I'll hurry home.

Better?"

I grip her face and bite her bottom lip. "Much fucking better, baby."

The person at the door knocks again. Smiling so damn hard that I feel as if my face is about to rip, I open the door and step out.

Kylie looks up at me and then at Riley, before grunting and motioning for me to get going. "About time. Damn! Your next client is here." She turns back to me. "Move along now."

Grabbing the back of Riley's neck, I pull her to me one more time and kiss her. "Love you, baby," I say, making sure that Kylie gets the fucking hint. "See you in a bit."

Rolling her eyes, Kylie storms past us and goes back to her desk without another word.

"Love you too." She slaps my ass and gives me a shove. "Now go, before I get fired."

I throw my hands up and start backing away. "Whoa now. Keep spanking me and I won't be going anywhere." I wink at her and then turn around to leave before I'm unable to stop myself.

Fuck me, I love this woman . . .

CHAPTER NINETEEN

Riley

TWO WEEKS LATER . . .

I'M STANDING IN FRONT OF the mirror when I feel Cale wrap his arms around me from behind. Like always when he's around, my heart starts pounding and I feel this rush. That feeling has only intensified since we have become official, and I seriously cannot get enough of him touching me.

"You look fucking beautiful, Rile." Grabbing my arm, he spins me around and whistles. "So damn beautiful."

Blushing, I wrap my arms around his neck and pull him down for a kiss. "Mmm . . ." I run my tongue over my lips, tasting the sweet strawberries that he just got done eating. "Save some of those for later," I say playfully. "If you keep eating them outside of the bedroom then we'll never have enough."

Grinning, he picks me up, wrapping my legs around his waist. His hands grab for my ass and squeeze. "Do we really have to go?" He questions, while pushing his erection against me. "I want to fuck my woman so bad right now that being with those assholes is the last thing on my mind. I'll call Slade back and tell him that we're not coming."

"No!" I scream as he starts rushing into the bedroom. "Don't do it, Cale." He stops in front of the bed and I grab onto his neck tighter, holding on for dear life. "We're going. We already said we would. My sister is waiting for me."

Growling against my lips, he wraps his hands into the back of my hair. "Well shit." He kisses me and smiles. "We don't have to stay long though, right? I've waited all damn day to get you home to me." He kisses me again, his lips lingering against mine. "Fine, let's go," he grumbles in defeat.

He sets me down to my feet and kisses the top of my head, before walking away and letting me finish getting ready.

The last two weeks have been the best days of my life and there's no denying it. Cale is so much more than I ever thought he could be. If I thought he made me feel special before, the feeling is double that now. This man hasn't let me go one second without a smile on my face and I have a feeling that if it's up to him then he'll never let that happen. Cale truly is the perfect man for me.

My love for him has grown so much that my chest aches just from being away from him. It keeps me happy knowing that he's always waiting for me, just like he used to before I left. It only proves to me exactly why he waited all these years for me. When Cale loves someone, he loves them with everything in him.

I'm just lucky to say that that girl is me.

Right as I'm in the middle of throwing my hair up, Cale rushes back into the bedroom and picks me up, throwing me over his shoulder. "I told you how beautiful you looked, Rile. You don't need to change anything. Trust me. Let's go!"

"I'm not done." I playfully slap his ass, but he keeps walking, not caring. "Damn you, Cale."

He doesn't set me down until we're outside next to his truck and he's opening the door for me. "We gotta go, baby. The sooner we get there, the sooner I get to bring you home and make love to you in our bed. I don't know how long I can hold off."

I bite my bottom lip and sit back in my seat as Cale shuts the door behind me and then runs over to his side of the truck.

I swear I have to be the luckiest girl in the world to have Cale. My Cale . . .

AS SOON AS WE STEP inside the bar, Stone jumps up on his chair and starts whistling for us to come over. "Dude! Over here."

I laugh as Hemy reaches over and punches him the leg. These guys will never change, and oddly, I'm good with that. Even though they drive me insane half the time, they're like family to me. No fuck that . . . they *are* family to me.

Now that I have Riley back here with me, my family is complete. There's no better feeling in the world than that. Tyler has gone back to Mexico where he belongs and Riley is here with me, where she has always belonged.

Placing my hand on Riley's ass, I guide her toward the table in the back and whisper in her ear. "Remember . . . we're not staying long. I'm spending the night pleasuring my fucking woman."

I see her cheeks turn red from my words, but she plays it off as Aspen walks over to her and hugs her, pulling her away from me and over to where her and Sage are playing darts.

Pulling out a chair, I take a seat next to Slade, across from Hemy and Stone. "What the fuck, dudes? Stop looking at me like that."

Slade tilts back his beer and grins like an idiot. "I just can't get over it, man. Shit." He takes another drink of his beer, before sliding one over to me. "One day we will be related."

"Ah, fuck." I grab my beer and bring it to my lips. "Ain't that some shit." I smile and nudge his shoulder. "Related to the fucking man whore. I never in a million years would've thought that could be a possibility. Shit is changing, man. Things are becoming real."

Hemy slaps Onyx on the ass as she stands up, nods at me, and goes to join the other girls. "So what's the deal," Hemy asks, before finishing his beer and pushing it aside. "Heard you punched the fuck out of Lynx and quit."

I nod my head and steel my jaw at just the thought of him trying to steal my woman out from under me. "Yeah, man. He had it coming."

"Hell yeah, he did," Stone agrees, tilting his beer to mine. "That asshole deserved it. Now he's all going crazy and shit, trying to find someone as good as you to take your spot. I mean Kash has been doing pretty good, but I don't know about this Stax guy. He looks scared as shit. The vultures smell fear. They may very well eat him alive."

Everyone around the table laughs. It's crazy how much things have changed over the last few months. I'm proud of every single guy at this table. I've never seen any of them happier than what they are right now, and I know for damn sure that I can now say that about myself as well.

Next week I start my management position at *The Anchor*, a bar that Riley and I can feel comfortable with me working at until I can decide what I really want to do. Slade is settling into his stiff new office job, wearing his suits and shit, Hemy has quit completely at *Walk Of Shame* and is working full time at his buddy's mechanic shop. I even heard that Onyx is getting a job with Aspen at the salon and that Sage is working on writing a book or something. Everything in life is fucking good to me. My people are good and so am I.

When I look over at the girls, I catch Riley smiling and looking back over at me while talking to Onyx about something. It makes me feel so damn good seeing her getting accepted by everyone in the group. I even have a feeling that Onyx finds her attractive. As wild as that girl is sometimes, I wouldn't be surprised if she hasn't thought about being with my girl. Of course there is one wild couple out of every group. Hemy and Onyx are that for us.

Grabbing my beer, I sit back in my seat and just enjoy this moment for what it is. This is the only group that I would want to be doing this with. My *Walk Of Shame* family became my real family, and I love all these fuckers to death.

This is all that a man needs to be happy. She is all a man needs to be happy. With these people, my life is fucking perfect . . .

THE END

Read on for special BONUS CONTENT

BONUS CONTENT

ONE YEAR LATER

TODAY HAS BEEN FILLED WITH endless phone calls, meetings and bullshit, yet all I can think about is getting home to my woman and hearing her moan beneath me. She's been on my mind all damn day, making it impossible to concentrate on all my cases.

Finally getting a chance to relax after a ten hour day, I loosen my tie, spin my chair away from my desk and bite my bottom lip in need when Aspen's sexy voice comes through the speaker of my office phone. Hearing her is exactly what I need to remember that my life isn't shit anymore.

"Hey, baby . . . you there?" She sighs when I don't respond, probably aware of the sound of my pants slowly unzipping. Might as well take this as a time to get comfortable and tease her at the same time. "What are you doing, Slade? Was that your zipper? Please tell me that was not the sound of your pants coming undone."

"If that's what you heard, then that was definitely my fucking zipper, baby."

Smiling to myself, I slide my hand into the waistband of my boxer briefs and grip my hard cock, getting harder by the second as Aspen's breathing picks up, working me up.

"Slade, you asshole. Are you seriously teasing me right now? That's not cool."

"You miss my hard cock, baby?" I loosen my tie some more and roll up my sleeves, getting more comfortable. "If you were here right now, I'd bend you over my fucking desk and fuck you so hard that the whole office building would get off on your screaming. How loud would you scream for me?"

I can tell by her loud breathing that she's completely sexually frustrated right now and fighting with everything in her not to explode. I love it. Makes my long work day more worthwhile when I get to come home to her. "Slade . . . leave that office and get your ass home. Now."

Smiling in victory, I run my tongue over my lips, wetting them. "Why?" I push.

She growls into the phone, not wanting to give in. She never wants to, but I'm working on that. "Slade . . ."

"Tell me," I demand.

"So you can fuck me. Dammit, you play dirty. This doesn't count. You know my weakness."

Standing up, I zip up my fly and start gathering up my all my shit. I swear I can't get out of this stuffy office soon enough. "It definitely counts. I'll be there in ten. Be ready."

Before Aspen can respond, I hit end on the phone call and rush out the door, locking it on the way out.

I don't even bother looking anywhere but straight ahead of me as I make my way through the building and outside to the parking lot. The last thing I need right now is someone thinking that I want to stop and chat. Not when my woman has finally broken down first. She's getting it. Fucking hard and dirty.

Just as I said, I pull up in the driveway of our new house, ten minutes later. I might have even ran a couple stop signs.

Not even bothering to grab my crap, I step out of my car, undoing my tie completely on the way to the front door.

I can barely even contain myself when I push the door open to see Aspen leaning over the kitchen island, wearing nothing but a thong and a very tight tank top. I can tell by the way that she doesn't even bother to look at me that she's reading one of Sage's books. Well that book is about to be put on hold until further fucking notice.

"Fuck me . . ." I step up behind her and run my hands along the curve of her ass, causing her to close her book and lean her head back to lay on my shoulder. "Everything in this house is brand new, yet you're the only thing I want to play with."

Gripping the counter, she perks her ass up, rubbing it against my cock. "Is that so?" she questions with a sexy growl. She rubs her ass in a circle, before turning to face me and gripping ahold of my shirt, tugging me closer to her. She knows that I'm on the verge of exploding and is taking this opportunity to torture me, but I guarantee that she will still be caving first.

She undoes the top two buttons on my black dress shirt, before biting her lip and walking over to pull out one of our new kitchen chairs. Her heated eyes stay on me the whole time. "There's a little something that I've been missing from you, Slade." Taking a seat in the chair, she spreads her legs and grips the seat between her thighs, looking sexy as sin. "Strip," she demands. "Nice and slow."

I feel my cock twitch from her demand. I love the playful Aspen and it's been a long time since I've been able to strip for her. This is bound to do the trick. She may not admit it, but this is how I got her in the first place.

Steeling my jaw, I yank her chair so that she's sitting right in front of me. It's time to get serious now. You ask Slade Merrick to strip . . . and you'll get a damn good show. "You asked for it."

Pulling my phone from my pocket, I scroll through to the music and hit play on the first slow song that I come across. To me it's not about the music; it's about how you move to it and I'm about to give her a glimpse into the Slade that she fell in love with.

After I set my phone down, I look her directly in the eye, making her squirm in her seat, as I empty my keys and everything else out of my pants. I don't want anything poking her except for my cock.

Biting my bottom lip, I step in between Aspen's legs and grip the top of her chair, grinding my hips as I work on undoing the rest of my shirt buttons.

Once I get to the last button, I yank my shirt off and toss it aside, before gabbing her hands and running them along my chiseled chest.

Moving in closer, I take a seat on her lap, grinding my hips to the slow rhythm. I can already see her starting to crumble and come undone beneath me. She wants this just as badly as I do.

"Slade . . ." she says in a shaky voice.

"Yes," I push. "What?" I move her hands lower, until she's stroking the length of my hardness through my dress pants.

She swallows hard and looks up to meet my gaze. "This is too damn hot and you know it . . ." she pauses as I stand up and start to undo my belt.

"You want me to keep going, baby?" After undoing my pants, I slide my hand down the front of my pants and stroke my cock with a moan. "I can keep going . . . or I can fuck you. What do you want?"

Aspen's legs slowly close and her grip on the chair tightens when I start to remove my pants. "I can do this," she whispers. "Stay strong."

Removing my pants completely, I stroke myself for her to watch, knowing that she can never handle when I touch myself. I give it less than two minutes.

"I'm so fucking hard, Aspen." I walk forward, stopping right in front of her. "I'll let you touch it . . . just say it."

Letting out a deep breath, Aspen growls, before reaching out and grabbing me by my cock. "I'm done. You win. I'm the first one to ask for sex in our new house. There. Happy?"

Wrapping a hand into the back of her hair, I pull her up to her feet and suck her bottom lip into my mouth. "Extremely fucking happy."

Pressing my lips to hers, I walk until we're back by the kitchen island, where she was when I first walked in. Then in one movement, I spin her around and bend her over the counter, slapping her ass with my free hand.

"It feels good, baby," I moan into her ear. "I'm about to fuck you in the house that we own together. It's you and me. This is just the beginning of our life together." Wrapping my arm around her neck, I pull her back so that I can kiss her. "I love you."

She smiles and licks her lips. "I love you too. Now hurry before I go crazy. It's already been three days."

I laugh because I love that we've only gone three days without having sex and this woman . . . my woman, already misses me inside of her. I never would've thought that day would come when I first met her over a year ago. It hardly feels like a month has passed.

Every day with her feels fresh and new and I couldn't be happier.

Unable to hold back any longer, I yank her panties aside and enter her wet pussy in one hard thrust, making her scream out from the intrusion.

"Slade!" Her breathing picks up as she waits for me to move. "I can't take this. Do you see how sexy you are in those damn suits? No more teasing. I. Want. You."

"Anything you want is yours." With that, I pull out and thrust back into her, causing her to moan out as I continue to take her deep and hard.

I'm rough at first, before slowing down and being gentle to remind her how much she means to me. This woman is everything to me and I never want her to forget.

It's not long before I feel her clenching around me, bringing me to my own orgasm as well. I push inside of her as deep as I can, giving her every last drop of me.

"Well the new house is broken in." I laugh into her ear, before kissing her neck, trailing my way around to her lips. "Now I never want to wait three days again. I was so fucking close to caving in."

"Are you serious?" She pulls away from me and spins around to face me. "How close?"

I smile and bite her bottom lip. "About ten minutes close." Gently, I press my lips against hers and catch her hands with mine. "Now go take a shower and I'll make you dinner."

"Slade . . ." she starts.

"Go," I say sternly. "You've taken time off work to help put our home together. Making dinner for my woman is the least I can do as a man." I tilt my head toward the hallway. "Hurry."

Shaking her head in disbelief, she smiles, before kissing me long and hard. "Never change," she whispers, then walks away, leaving me alone to clean up a bit and cook dinner.

ASPEN APPEARS FROM THE SHOWER about twenty five minutes later, dressed in one of my white button down shirts. She takes one look at me by the stove, in my boxers, and growls.

"This might just be sexier than seeing you in a suit. Almost naked, cooking. I dig it," she teases.

Running my hands through my hair, I look at her and feel like the luckiest man in the world as I watch her take a seat in our kitchen.

I've been wanting to ask her to buy a place with me for months now, but I wanted to make sure it was the right time. Last week when I watched her walk out the door for work, I realized that I never wanted her to come back home to a place that wasn't ours together. I knew right then that the time was right. I'm just lucky that she has as much faith in me as she does.

Sometimes I feel as if I don't deserve it, but she always finds a way to remind me just how much she thinks I do. When the time is right, I will make her my wife and I will love her with everything in me. I may have had a hard past, but I'm ready for a new future and I know without a doubt that future is her . . . Aspen.

"I'm the luckiest asshole in the world," I admit.

Aspen walks into my open arms and smiles against my chest as I hug her to me. "Yeah . . . and you're my asshole. I'm not giving you up for anything."

I feel Aspen jump in my arms as my phone starts vibrating next to us. Looking over, I see Hemy's name flash across the screen. "Shit . . ." That's tonight.

Reaching for my phone, I answer it and grunt, before speaking.

"Yeah, man."

"Don't forget, dude. We're meeting Cale and Riley at Walk Of Shame in two hours. Don't be late again."

I hear some loud noise in the background and Onyx cheering, before the phone goes silent. Sounds like they're at the club already. No surprise there.

Tossing my phone down, I kiss Aspen on the top of the head. "Looks like we have a couple of hours . . ." I lift my eyebrows in suggestion and Aspen slaps my chest.

"We'll see how good dinner is," she teases.

I may sound like a pussy, but my heart skips a beat from the sight of her smile. I'll never grow tired of seeing it every day.

I'll never grow tired of us. Slade and Aspen. She is exactly where I need to be and I'm going to show her in every way that I can . . .

Hemy

I HUNG UP WITH SLADE over an hour ago, and Onyx has been pushing me ever since to go show the new guys how it's really done. She said the idea of me being back here makes her want to jump all over me and take me for a ride. Well fuck me . . .

I have to admit that watching the guys sort of has me wanting to go up on the stage and show them what's up, just for the fucking rush.

Peeling my eyes away from the stage, I cup Onyx's face in my hands and pull her in for a rough kiss. All I need is five fucking minutes to show these dicks how it's really done. "Fuck it," I say with a smirk. "I'll be back."

Taking a quick swig of my drink, I slam it down and make my way over to where Kash is dancing. This is sure to get his ass laid at least.

Stepping up behind Kash, I push him forward, stopping him right in front of the sexy little blonde that has been eyeing him up and down ever since he stepped on the stage.

Leaning in to his ear, I whisper, "Make love to her fucking face. Show her what you can do." I slap his back and wink at the girl as she grins at me.

Kash gives me a look as if he's uncertain if he should do it or not. "Seriously, dude?"

"Fuck . . ." Grabbing the back of the girl's neck, I slowly push her down to her knees in front of him. "Grab the back of her head." I place my hand on the eager girl's chin, making her look up at me. "You want this?"

She smiles at me before turning back to Kash and looking

up at him with a sexy grin. Her eyes are practically begging for his cock in her face. "Very much. Kash . . ."

Kash runs his tongue over his lips, before reaching down and gripping the back of the girl's neck, slowly thrusting his hips to the music.

Stepping behind the girl, I grab her hands to guide her, placing one on Kash's ass and the other on the button of his jeans.

So much better . . .

"Fuck . . . that shit isn't hard," I mutter while making my way back over to where Onyx is waiting for me.

When I take a seat, I am taken by surprise when Onyx jumps into my lap, pressing me into the back of the leather couch.

With a grin, she wraps her hand around my neck and leans down to whisper in my ear. "I'm extremely hot right now, Hemy." She bites my earlobe before releasing it. "Do you know why?"

Gripping her hips, I lift her up, pulling her as close to me as humanly possible. Then I grip the back of her neck and yank her face to mine, brushing my lips over hers. "Because you're in my lap," I say with confidence. Getting turned on, I thrust my hips into her, showing her just how hard I am. "And because of my newest piercing."

She runs her tongue over her lips, seductively and nods her head. "Bingo!" Reaching in between us, she grabs my cock through my jeans and squeezes. "And that fucking man bun turns me on. It makes me want to do very naughty things . . ."

Swallowing hard, I lace my fingers with hers and lean in, pressing my lips against the ring on her left hand. Seeing that rock, gets me both excited and extremely turned on, knowing that this woman has agreed to be my wife.

"Fuck . . . I love it when my fiancé wants to be naughty." Yanking her to her feet, I stand up and walk her backward, until we're lost in a dark corner, away from the loud screaming by the stage. I just hope that Stone and Kash can keep the room busy long enough so I can please my woman and finally test out this new piercing.

Slamming Onyx against the wall, I slide my hand up the front of her skirt, shoving a finger inside of her already wet pussy. "So fucking wet, baby," I whisper against her neck, about to lose my shit.

Moaning, she throws her head back as I begin to pump my fingers inside of her.

"Faster, Hemy," she demands.

I shake my head and pull my fingers out, sucking them into my mouth. "Nah . . ." Reaching in between us, I pull my cock out of my jeans, faster than I ever have in my entire life. Not being able to have sex without a condom for the past five weeks has been making me crazy to be inside of her again.

Before Onyx can react from my cock being out, I grip her leg, wrap it around my waist and slam into her. Deep and hard.

I feel her nails dig into my back as I still myself inside of her. "Fuck, Hemy!" She screams next to my ear. "Why do you have to be so big?" She takes a few deep breaths to compose herself. "I can take it," she breathes. "Go."

Cupping her chin, I force her to look up at me. "You okay, baby?" My eyes lock with hers, searching for the truth. "I didn't mean to hurt you, but fuck . . . I can't hold back right now."

"Don't," she breathes. She squeezes me with her leg to get me moving again. "Just a little warning next time so I can prepare. Now move before I go crazy."

Grinning, I wrap one hand around her throat and grab onto her leg with my free hand. "Here's your warning . . ."

I pull out and slam back into her, causing her to dig her nails into the back of my neck and scream out. "Keep going," she breathes.

Resting my forehead to hers, I begin to pound into her, fast and hard, giving her everything that I have. With this woman, I can't hold back. She drives me fucking wild in the best possible way. She always has and that's exactly why I asked her to marry me a few months ago. The truth is, I can't live without this woman. I've tried it once and barely survived. I won't do it again.

The faster I go, the louder her breathing becomes, showing me just how close she is to coming undone. As much as I want to make this last, everyone will be here soon and the last thing we need is for them to come looking for us.

"Yeah, baby," I growl into her ear. "Come for me. You feel that?" I sway my hips in a circle, letting her feel every last inch of my cock.

She nods her head and digs her teeth into her bottom lip. "Just a little bit," she says breathless.

I squeeze her thigh tighter and push in even deeper, before slowly pulling all the way out. "Now?" I ask again.

"Yes," she moans. "Fuck, I love your cock and the rings. All of it Hemy. I love all of you."

I can never grow tired of hearing those words from her lips. When I come home from a long day at the shop, she's always right there, telling me how much she loves me.

Nothing can ever compare to that and I make sure that my body and actions always show her that. She is the only one that I want. The only one I've ever wanted.

I slam into her and stop. "I love all of you too, beautiful." I pull out and thrust back into her, stopping to kiss her lips. "Especially because you love this so much. Now hold on."

Understanding what's coming, she holds onto me as tightly as she can and leans her head into my shoulder.

Gripping her thigh for support, I bury my face into her neck and fuck her fast and hard, not stopping until we've both reached orgasm, her screaming upon release in my ear.

I press my forehead to hers and smile in satisfaction as we look into each other's eyes. "I love you so fucking much. Never forget that, got it?"

Onyx nods her head and runs her hands through the loose strands of my hair. "I love you too." She lifts her hand with the ring. "Always."

"Good," I say in relief. Stepping away from her, I pull my shirt over my head and clean Onyx of her light sheen of sweat, before cleaning myself off and tossing it into the nearest trash can.

"Let's get back before the group shows up." Grabbing Onyx's hand, I pull her against me and walk us back through the crowd and to our area by the couches. The V.I.P section is ours for the night and I have to admit that it feels nice being back here, knowing that the whole group will be here soon.

Right as we're about to sit down, my phone starts vibrating in my pocket. I don't even have to look at it to know who it is. Cale has been on our asses for the last week, making sure that every one of us is here tonight at nine.

It's a little past eight, so I don't know what his deal is. Have a little faith in us, damn.

I pull my phone out and answer it without even bothering to look at the screen. "We're already here, man. And I called Slade about an hour ago and reminded him."

"You're there?" Cale questions. "Is everything good there?"

I let out a small breath and look around the bar at everyone having a good time. The guys are shaking their dicks and the women are having the time of their fucking lives. He worries too damn much. "Yeah, man. It's all good here. No worries. We'll see ya soon."

Right as I'm hanging up, Onyx jumps from her seat on the couch and runs over to greet Sage. Those two have become inseparable and I have to say that it makes me extremely happy.

Onyx has been treating her like a sister for longer than I have and if anyone ever hurts her, I have a feeling that Onyx would get to them before I would even have a chance to.

"Love the hair," Sage says, while grabbing a handful of Onyx's hair.

Ever since Onyx has been working at the salon with Aspen, she has been experimenting with different hairstyles and colors. I have to say that this is my favorite so far. It's almost black, but looks purple in some lighting. It's fucking sexy on her.

Giving me a quick hug, Sage pulls away and walks her way up to the stage to greet Stone. It's as if the screaming, groping girls has no effect on her. She just pushes right through them, wraps an arm around Stone's neck and slams her lips against his, showing them who he's going home with tonight.

It's been a year and those two have managed to stay friends with benefits. Sage says it's what she wants at the moment, but I have to admit that it still drives me crazy. He just better hope that he never hurts her. I'd hate to have to break his pretty face. Well maybe . . .

Stone sees me looking up at him as Sage walks away, making her way back over to us. Stone throws up his middle fingers and sticks his tongue out while thrusting the air. Fast.

"Fucking dick," I grumble.

I feel a bony fist hit me in the ribs. "Be nice, big brother." Sage bites her lip and winks over at Stone. "He's so fucking cute. How can you be so mean to him?"

"It's not too hard. Trust me," I growl out.

"Oh stop it," Onyx jumps in, like the big sister to protect Sage. "Try to have some fun instead of bitching over Stone. You spend over nine hours a day busting your ass on those cars and crap. Loosen up. No worries."

Sage smiles at Onyx before turning to me and wrapping her arm around my neck. "Yeah, what she said big bro. It could be worse," she teases. "I could ask you to read one of my books." She smiles real big at me, knowing that I hate the idea of that.

"I've heard the shit you write and there's no way in hell I'm going to read about your sexual adventures."

Onyx and Sage both slap me at the same time. I just smile because I'm used to it. This is my life now. These women are my life.

I grip my beer and sit back and relax as the girls fall into some deep girl talk conversation. This somehow makes me wish that the assholes would hurry up and get here, but then I look over and notice the smile on both of their faces and I fall apart like a fucking pussy.

I have the two most important women in my life here and will be damned if I ever mess that up . . .

Cale

LACING MY FINGERS WITH RILEY'S, I lean in and smile against her lips, before kissing her soft and deep. I can never get tired of tasting this woman's lips. Especially after waiting as long as I did. I never want to wait again.

Her legs tighten around me as I thrust into her, quickening my speed. The way that she squeezes me, pushes me in even deeper, making me about ready to lose my shit right now.

Truthfully, I should have lost it over ten minutes ago. I've been on everyone's ass to make sure that they aren't late tonight, yet here I am still making love to wife.

Being inside of her, hearing her soft moans as I bury myself between her thighs is all that matters at the moment. Here with her is where I belong.

"Cale . . ." She digs her nails into my back and moans as her body starts trembling from below me. I love feeling her come undone because of me. "Oh my goodness . . . Oh my . . ."

Thrusting into her a few more times, I push in deep, releasing myself inside of her. "Fuck me, baby."

Wrapping my arms around her, I roll over, pulling her on top of me. "You're so damn beautiful." I wrap my hands into the back of her hair and pull her in for a kiss. "You know that, right?"

Smiling as if she's the happiest woman in the world, she nods and presses little kisses into my neck. "You never let me forget." She kisses me one more time, before pulling back and running her hand through my hair. "Everyone's going to hate us. You know that, right? By the time we get there, we're going to be over thirty minutes late."

Sucking my bottom lip into my mouth, I grip Riley's ass, lifting her up and off of me. "They won't hate us for long. Trust me." I slap her ass as she stands up, causing her to yelp and look back at me. "I love you," I say to soften her up.

Shaking her head, she smiles and starts walking backward, toward the bathroom. "Dammit! I love you too, but not so rough next time. Especially when we can't stay home and play." She winks at me and then disappears into the bathroom to get ready.

We pull up in the parking lot of Walk Of Shame thirty minutes later, us both rushing out of the car. In a hurry, Riley speeds up, walking ahead of me, but I grab her arm, slowing her down.

Whistling, I spin her around, checking her out in her little black dress. "Perfection."

She gets that look on her face that she's gotten for the last eleven years whenever I do this and it brings me back to the beginning, reminding me exactly why I fell in love with her in the first place.

"Cale . . ." She slaps my chest and I spin her into my chest, pulling her in for a kiss. "Let's go." I kiss her again, not wanting to let her go. "God, you're so adorable," she breathes, "But we need to hurry. I'm so anxious!"

Placing my hand on the small of her back, I guide her to the door and inside to where the crew is waiting in the V.I.P section. The first person I spot is Slade.

He nods at me and then hits Hemy in the side, letting him know that we've arrived. I can already see them talking shit about us being late and it only makes me want to laugh. Those two are usually never on time so fuck it.

Sara and Jules wave at us from behind the bar, letting me know that they're fine. Eight months ago, Lynx had some shit go down and Hilary took the club away from him. I was the first person that she asked to take over. I was hesitant at first, but let the fact that most of the people here are my family, talk me into agreeing.

Stone, Kash, Styx, Sara and now Jules have become a big part of our crew and if I can help them out in any way, then that's what I plan on doing. Plus it's good money and we're definitely going to need it now . . .

"Look who's late," Slade says with a sly grin. "Good thing I took my time getting here."

"Ass." I slug him on the shoulder and take a seat on the couch, pulling Riley down with me.

As soon as Lila sees us join the group, she rushes over to take our drink order.

"Just a beer." I hand her a twenty, before she turns to take Riley's order. Unfortunately, it's going to give everything away.

"I'll take a water," she says softly.

Almost everyone in the group stops what they are doing and turns to gawk at us.

"You're pregnant," Onyx shouts. "Aren't you!"

Lila whisper, "Congratulations," to Riley, before walking away to grab our drinks.

"Dude," Slade pushes.

"Well?" Aspen chimes in. "Tell us!"

Standing up, I pull Riley up with me, placing my hand over her belly. "Eight weeks," I say with the biggest smile on my face. "Looks like we're adding a new addition to our family, guys."

Everyone watches me in awe as I drop to my knees and kiss Riley's belly. My baby is in the woman that I love. Our baby.

"Well . . ." Riley says nervously. "Say something. You guys are too damn quiet."

Aspen bursts into tears while reaching out to pull Riley into her arms. "I'm going to be an aunt." Being sure not to hurt Riley, she shakes her, pulling her in as tight as she can. "Holy shit! I'm going to be an aunt, guys!"

Jumping to his feet, Slade throws his arms around the both of them and kisses the top of their heads. Then he reaches over and grabs the back of my head. "Congrats, man. I'm so fucking happy for you guys."

I can see him fighting hard to hide his emotions. I know his past still hurts him, but the time will come for him and Aspen to start their own family. Hopefully soon. I know they're both ready.

Sage, Onyx, Hemy . . . everyone takes turns giving Riley a hug, showing their love and excitement. Seeing all the support from them almost brings tears to my eyes, but I fight it.

Somehow knowing that I'm about to have a baby has made me more emotional. It makes me more appreciative of the love and support we have, knowing that our child will have the same.

After all the excitement is done, everyone falls into conversation about whether or not it's going to be a girl or boy. Hemy and Slade actually make a bet on it. Hemy says a dude and Slade says a girl.

I'm happy either way. I just want to hold the love of our lives and show him or her how much we're going to love and take care of them.

Hemy holds up his drink, interrupting everyone. "You should all know that if it's a dude that he's going to take after uncle, Hemy. You should be so lucky."

All three of the girl's eyes go wide, before Onyx and Sage start talking at the same time about how badly that shouldn't happen.

"The girls don't need any more dirty boys like you Hemy," Onyx says, before whispering, "Only me," and winking.

Slade grips my shoulder and squeezes. "I'll take care of that child as if it were mine. Never forget that, bro. I love you, man."

I can feel the truth is Slade's words and it warms my heart. It's taken time, but Slade is one of the best men that I know. He's protective and gives his all. It makes me happy to know my kid will have an uncle like him. "Love you too, bro."

Riley and the girls are in the middle of a conversation, but I pick Riley up, pulling her into my lap. Knowing that she is carrying my child makes me want to be as close to her as possible. The truth is . . . I just may never let her go now.

Eleven years ago, she became my life. Seven months ago, she became my wife and now she'll become the mother of my children. I will always show her her worth and how much she means to me. My family will always come first.

Snuggling into my arms, she smiles against my neck as I place my hand over her stomach. "I love you, daddy," she says with a small laugh.

Pulling her face up to reach mine, I press my lips against hers and rest my forehead to hers. "I love you too, baby. Always have and always will. Never forget that."

She smiles and looks me in the eyes. I can see by the way she's looking at me that she knows it's the truth. I would never lie to her. "I know, baby. I've always known."

A few minutes later, I look up to see Stone dancing while watching us from across the room. He knows something is up.

Standing up, I pull Riley to her feet and place my hand over her stomach, like I have almost every day since we've found out.

Stone's eyes widen and a grin takes over his face. Without much thought, he hops off the stage and runs over to us.

"Holy shit!" Grabbing Riley's face, he presses a kiss to the top of her head, before turning to me and doing the same. "Congratu-fucking-lations. I knew it! You've been acting different, man. That's awesome."

He pulls me in for a one arm hug as I squeeze his shoulder, thankful to see he's just as excited as the rest of us. "Thank you, man." I pull away from him. "Now get back on the fucking stage." I smile, showing my appreciation as he rushes back over to the stage surrounded by a bunch of confused looking chicks. He doesn't even miss a beat, falling back into his routine.

Just wanting to be close to my wife, I pull her into my arms and kiss her long and deep, pretending that it's just the two of us. As much as I want to spend time with these guys . . . my family, the excitement of going home to work out the nursery is tugging at my heart. I don't think I'll be able to sleep until I know my baby is going to have the best fucking room ever.

Leaning over Riley's head, I grab Slade's shoulder. "Hey, man. I think we're going to get going."

He looks at me, searching my eyes. He knows that feeling. He knows what it's like to want to be the man and take care of things. It's too bad that he never got that opportunity. "You need any help man, let me know. Any free time that I have, you know you have Aspen and I. We're just a call away."

"I know, man." I squeeze his shoulder. "I'll definitely be calling too. Just not tonight, man. Now that everyone knows, the excitement of it all is kicking in. We have a lot of thinking to do."

"Hell yeah," Slade responds, before turning to Aspen and picking her up, pulling her to him. "I know the feeling." He kisses Aspen's neck and squeezes her as if he never wants to let her go. "One day, man. One day . . ."

When I look over to say bye to Hemy, he's standing with his arm around Onyx, them both laughing it up and talking to Sage as if there isn't a care in the world. I swear I hear baby talk.

In this moment, I know that everyone is right where they belong. Slade has the love of his life, a new home and a good job. Hemy has his fiancé, their home and I have my wife, a baby on the way and a business to run with the love of my life.

The Walk Of Shame family couldn't ask for anything better . . .

ACKNOWLEDGEMENTS

FIRST AND FOREMOST, I'D LIKE to say a big thank you to all my loyal readers that have given me support over the last couple years and have encouraged me to continue with my writing. Your words have all inspired me to do what I enjoy and love. Each and every one of you mean a lot to me and I wouldn't be where I am if it weren't for your support and kind words.

I'd also like to thank my friend, Author of the Fate Series and editor, Charisse Spiers. She has put a lot of time into helping me put this story together. I'm lucky to have her be a part of this journey with me. Please everyone look out for her books. She has shown me so much support through this whole process and it would be nice to be able to return the favor. Her stories are beautifully written and something that the world shouldn't miss out on.

My amazingly, wonderful PA, Amy Preston Rogers. She helped me from the very beginning of Cale and fell in love with him before anyone else. Her support has meant so much to me.

Also, all of my beta readers, both family and friends that have taken the time to read my book and give me pointers throughout this process. You guys have helped encourage me more than you know. *Bestsellers and Beststellars of Romance* for hosting my cover reveal, blog tour and release day blitz. Hetty Whitmore Rasmussen has been a big part in making this happen. You all have. Thank you all so much.

I'd like to thank another friend of mine, Clarise Tan from *CT Cover Creations* for creating my cover. You've been wonderful to work with and have helped me in so many ways.

Thank you to my boyfriend, friends and family for understanding my busy schedule and being there to support me through the hardest part. I know it's hard on everyone, and everyone's support means the world to me.

Last but not least, I'd like to thank all of the wonderful book bloggers that have taken the time to support my book and help spread the word. You all do so much for us authors and it is greatly appreciated. I have met so many friends on the way and you guys are never forgotten. You guys rock. Thank you!

ABOUT THE AUTHOR

VICTORIA ASHLEY GREW UP IN Rockford, IL and has had a passion for reading for as long as she can remember. After finding a reading app where it allowed readers to upload their own stories, she gave it a shot and writing became her passion.

She lives for a good romance book with tattooed bad boys that are just highly misunderstood and is not afraid to be caught crying during a good read. When she's not reading or writing about bad boys, you can find her watching her favorite shows such as Sons Of Anarchy, Dexter and True Blood.

She is the author of Wake Up Call, This Regret, Slade, Hemy, Get Off On The Pain and Thrust and is currently working on more works for 2015.

CONTACT HER AT:

www.victoriaashleyauthor.com
or on
Facebook
Twitter
Instagram

BOOKS BY VICTORIA ASHLEY

Wake Up Call
This Regret
Thrust

WALK OF SHAME
Slade (#1)
Hemy (#2)
Cale (#3)

PAIN
Get Off on the Pain
Something for the Pain (#2) Coming 2015

3 1333 04771 0817